Dana Kelleher Bost is on her fourth reincarnation, this time as a writer. She spent a decade traveling the backroads of Virginia as a visiting nurse, then a decade as a full-time mother of two boys and a part-time photographer, which led to a twenty-four-year stint as an English/Drama/Film teacher at a private school in Virginia. This is her first novel.

Dedicated to

HOPE

Dana Kelleher Bost

LAPHATTON

AUSTIN MACAULEY PUBLISHERS™

LONDON · CAMBRIDGE · NEW YORK · SHARJAH

Ordering Information
Quantity sales: Special discounts are available on quantity purchases by corporations, associations, and others. For details, contact the publisher at the address below.

Publisher's Cataloging-in-Publication data
Bost, Dana Kelleher
Laphatton

ISBN 9798886938784 (Paperback)
ISBN 9798886938791 (Hardback)
ISBN 9798886938807 (ePub e-book)

Library of Congress Control Number: 2023917449

www.austinmacauley.com/us

First Published 2024
Austin Macauley Publishers LLC
40 Wall Street, 33rd Floor, Suite 3302
New York, NY 10005
USA

mail-usa@ austinmacauley.com
+1 (646) 5125767

Chapter 1
Dysphoria

Harken knew he had to speak soon. If he didn't, he would be labeled a weirdo, so he mumbled a greeting to a few others and tried to look normal. He ached for the familiar and later that afternoon upon shutting his door, number 27, he paced about his six by twelve-foot cubicle trying to remain aware of his breath, his footfalls, his heartbeat. The fist in his chest gradually relaxed. His thumb and forefinger toyed with the satchel of coffee beans in his coat pocket. He worked one free and munched on it. Raucous voices rang out up and down the corridor, and he wished he could do the same.

Next door in number 25, Phoenix pulled a white rat out of her pack. She held it to her nose and took in its smell. Its pink ears stood straight up. Suddenly it leapt onto her face, found a foothold in her nose ring and then disappeared into the brim of her hat. Phoenix retrieved a dictionary printed in 1983, forty-seven years before the power turned off for good and opened to page 665. The word she sought was *Herodotus*: *n. 1. 484? – 425? BC Greek historian. 2. a crater in the second quadrant of the face of the moon; about*

23 miles in diameter. She looked out the dirty window at the moon and repeated the definition.

Across the hall in room number 22, Sol raised his right foot to rest on his left knee, turning it to investigate the splinter that ran deep into the pad beneath the big toe. He pressed on either side of the angry redness and let out a shriek. The splinter edged forward. He gritted his teeth and squeezed again. Ready for the pain this time, he rolled back onto his cot and chanted a favorite line from a story about a girl named Alice, "When a thing happens, you stand it whether you can or not." The splinter had to come out or he wouldn't survive tomorrow, the first day of camp.

Fifteen children, ages twelve to fourteen, lay down on their cots. Some studied the cracks in the ceiling, some fell asleep easily and some listened to the building, a crumbling ruin of what was once a Smallpox Hospital located on Roosevelt Island, New York.

All night the moon pulled the tide up the East River. The restless wind chattered around the island, stirring up trash and irritating the monkeys who huddled in the few remaining trees. The monkeys were descendants of the island hospital's lab chimps who were set free when the electrical grids went down for good, and the internet went dark forever. Mankind, steeped in arrogance and greed, almost destroyed the planet.

The population that survived struggled in a lawless land of rival groups. The year was 2064, thirty-four years after the first missiles were fired and still, it was chaos. The monkeys, unlike humans who could escape the island, were hemmed in by the river. Twenty or so eked out a miserable existence, and no one bothered them. In fact, until today, no one came to Roosevelt Island at all, and the three inhabitants who did live there were in for a surprise. Now, the island had its first visitors since before the war, sent here for survival training, and the camp director knew just what to do. Nothing.

Chapter 2
Impunity

On the other end of the island, the infamous Octagon Asylum sat in ruin staring out at Manhattan with its dark eyes. Exposed to the weather, its medical equipment had become a sculpture garden of rusted abstract art. Before the war, the most difficult patients wandered its halls. All had committed serious crimes: murder, fraud, grand larceny. Conditions there were dreadful, and the staff was known to be brutal. Ironically, the downfall of the modern world set those imprisoned in the Octagon Asylum free. Most disappeared into the chaos on the mainland, but some remained and like every other species, produced offspring.

Garnal, one of the three island residents, shoved a rag into the crack below his glass door. He was colder than usual and wrapped himself in another blanket. Outside, the gas pumps stood glistening. He found it comforting to look at them. The station had been his home now for twenty-eight years if he had kept track. There was a blue Volvo sedan permanently parked at the pumps and a Mercury Marquis pulled into the far bay where he slept. Tonight, he was jumpy. He had seen a boat approach the island and discharge what looked like a lot of people.

His hand shook slightly as he retrieved the key ring from its hook and with short, shuffling steps, he scurried from lock to lock. Once secured, he stood and like countless others from the beginning of time, gazed up at the moon and wondered. Then he turned, hung the keys on their hook and slid into the Mercury Marquis driver's seat. He hit the lock button and listened for the reassuring click. Now, he could sleep.

As she did every night, Cedar checked to see if Garnal's door was locked. *Safe,* she thought. Cedar had just turned thirteen, if she had known her actual birthday, but birthdays were a thing of a decadent past. In her small world of three, Cedar set her own rules. Hunger drove her. Tonight, she hopped on her bicycle, a rattletrap of unfamiliar parts, and headed down the moonlit path that led to the old hospital ruin to see if she had netted anything off the pier. If so, she would share the feast with Garnal and Slacker, the third and oldest island resident.

The reliable moon did its job lighting her way. Cedar flew. She stood on the pedals and held her arms outstretched. The wind tasted of rain. Her sandy brown hair was long and tangled into explosive clumps that had no plan. She was a modern-day hunter-gatherer who survived by her wits. Too young by pre-war standards to be crawling about with a knife in her mouth, but the day of the sheltered childhood was over.

The predator in her felt something in the air, and she slowed to a crawl. All her senses relayed danger and just then, she spotted the source. A boat bobbed in the river, and there was movement near the hospital ruin.

Quickly, she hid the bike and clambered up one of the few surviving trees. What was happening on her island? She decided to settle in for the night, close enough to see it all.

Chapter 3
Servitude

The next morning at 5:00 AM, the camp director strode up the steps and marched into the dormitory hallway. His sharply curved beak-like nose and pointy chin almost touched. He was disappointed to see just one recruit up and ready, Phoenix. She was always early, always the first, always prepared. It drove some people crazy, but she didn't care. Why not be first? She knocked on Sol's door just as the camp leader stuck four dirty fingers between his thin lips and let out a shrieking whistle.

Phoenix jumped, and the remaining doors flew open. Suddenly, the hall was full of poorly clad, greasy haired children of all shapes and sizes. Poor hygiene was a way of life now, and this generation knew nothing first-hand about the daily shower of days gone by. Everyone was talking at once until four filthy fingers once again produced a fireworks of shrieks. Spit flew, and the recruits fell silent. Slowly, he did a 360 degree turn and stared into their eyes.

"I hope you are ready for Survival Challenge Week!" He paused dramatically. "You don't look ready. In fact, you look quite dull to me, and there is no place for dull here. How many here have been to some kind of school?" Hands went up, seven. The director sighed. "How many can read?" All hands went up. *Maybe that's what set them apart,* he thought. "Report to the courtyard immediately!" he barked, and the hall emptied out.

The director stretched to his full height of six feet and followed them outside. The recruits stood in silence, but their presence had set the monkeys chattering, and above them all perched Cedar watching, counting, listening, calculating. Her stomach growled, and she punched it. There was no catch in her net last night.

Harken sat leaning against the tree just below Cedar. She stared at the top of his head. He had thick dark hair curled into loose ringlets that bobbed like worms. Cedar wanted to touch them.

Spread out across the courtyard, the students stood in nervous circles that changed sizes. The man in charge appeared with a large wooden box. He set it on the ground, and they all gathered around. The strange box had a shiny silver crank on one side. All were silent as he leaned over the mysterious offering and opened the lid which produced a circular platform that rose up. Then the platform began to spin as the camp director turned the crank. Next, he lifted what looked like a silver arm and placed it on the spinning disk.

His captive audience surrendered to the sound of piano keys struck a hundred years ago and recorded on what was called vinyl. No one here had heard a record played before nor had any campers ever touched a piano. The notes spun between them and then up into the trees, and then up into the gray sky.

The melody began slowly like a beggar pleading on her knees for help. The notes, soft at first, cradled them and then they grew in speed and force until it felt like the music might lift them up into the clouds. The circle was transfixed.

Meanwhile, the man with the pointy face retreated into the building without a word. The children listened. The wind changed direction, the sun rose higher in the sky, and the earth continued to rotate on its axis. The spinning disk slowed, and the music wound down and stopped.

The circle of children remained frozen in place, unsure of what this meant or what to do. The moment stretched on and on until Phoenix stepped into the silence. She pushed back her excuse for a hat and leaned down to examine the box. She read, *"Rachmaninoff piano concerto #3."* She stood with her hands on her hips, "I'll look that up, maybe it's a clue." Just then, Ratty stuck his head up out of her shirt pocket and set the circle laughing.

Chapter 4
Look It Up

Phoenix sat at the center of the circle and tugged her beloved dictionary out of her pack. She started with the name, *Rachmaninoff* and read aloud: *"Sergei 1873-1943: Russian composer, conductor and pianist."* Questions arose. She held up a finger asking her new campmates to be patient as she moved on to the words: *conductor* and *composer* and read the definitions out loud. Confusion set in as her peers debated the possible meanings. How would this help them learn to be resilient survivors and leaders for the future?

Phoenix flipped through the pages, and her eyes wandered to the word *musing*. She sat and read, *adj. 1. absorbed in thought, meditative.* She was reading about what she was doing. Pleased, she looked up just as the circle around the music box exploded into arms and legs going in every direction. A dark blur grabbed the box by the crank and was dragging it off. "Shit, it's a monkey!" she blurted out. The words hung in the air. All eyes turned to her. Surprised by her unlikely outburst, she immediately retreated into her book to look up *monkey* even though she knew this one by heart because it had a picture. The circle dissolved.

A boy limped over to Phoenix and sat down. "Can I have a look?"

"Maybe."

"Look up infection for me, would ya?" The skinny boy ripped his right shoe off and pushed on a bright red spot. "I got the splinter out but it hurts like wacko."

"You shouldn't tell anyone. They'll throw you out," whispered Phoenix. She leaned toward him to smell the wound. Ratty squirmed his way out of her pocket and sniffed at the puffy footpad too. Above them, a nervous wind rattled the leaves. Phoenix thought it sounded like a conversation. Unaware of the spy above him, Sol worked at his infection as images of his parents flitted at the edge of his consciousness. He shut them out and turned his attention to his fellow camp competitors.

Meanwhile, Cedar measured and graded them all from her elevated view and wondered why they had come to her island. She felt sorry for the skinny boy and thought she should help him. The boy leaning on her tree seemed interesting, but most of all, she wanted to know why the girl with the rat liked that book so much. Cedar couldn't read.

She had so many questions but was unsure how to proceed. *Slow and steady wins the race*, she thought to herself. These words of wisdom came from Slacker, her substitute parental unit. He would not be happy with this small invasion. Cedar wondered about Garnal's reaction to the strangers. She thought she better let him know about the visitors and help him adjust. She needed to get moving.

Chapter 5
Congenital

Garnal was up at sunrise as always. He did the same thing every day and in the same order. First, he turned the black knobs on the Mercury's dashboard back to the right. Second, he exited the gas station from the rear and relieved himself in the tall weeds. Then he re-entered the station, locked the door and waited for Cedar. If Cedar showed up, he would go outside and sit between the towers to watch for the monkeys or go treasure hunting.

Garnal lived in the moment. He had no idea who his family was or where he came from. He didn't think about things like that. His parents, who worked as hospital orderlies, had fled the island when he was five and never looked back. His father was mildly handicapped due to anoxia at birth, and his mother had absolutely no conscience. She did as she pleased, including leaving Garnal behind.

Pre-war, Garnal would have been diagnosed as autistic, but as things stood now, he was just Garnal. He paced, he counted, he checked, he explored, and he collected shiny objects.

Unlike Garnal, Cedar was the direct descendant of a Honduran nurse and a Chilean research assistant working at the asylum for the summer. She had an IQ, if it could be measured, of 146. Her parents had been more attentive than Garnal's but had died when she was six of what she didn't know. The only adult on the island, Slacker, had stepped in and looked after her. He was a sweet man, reliable and compassionate. Slacker could read, but he wasn't a teacher and learning to read was a luxury at this point in time, so Cedar had taken on the task herself. The hospital library still had shelves of books, and so far, she had isolated the twenty-six symbols that made up the words.

Then she heard Phoenix speak, "Infection is a noun and means an infecting with germs of disease." She stared at Sol, "That's not very helpful." Phoenix's family came from a long line of Irish tinkers or gypsies well known for their ability to heal and to adapt. Her parents thought that she showed great promise. They taught her to read, simple math and science, and how to sew. At the bottom of her pack was a tin of needles and two spools of thread. Her dictionary was her most prized possession.

Sol dropped his foot and squeezed it back into a filthy sneaker. "Yeah, I already knew that." For him, this splinter was infection number 86. He liked to keep track of how many and where he got each one.

Unbeknownst to him, he was a direct descendant of a royal line of tribal leaders in West Anglia who were kidnapped by slavers in 1700 and sold to a plantation in South Carolina. His parents adored him, but they struggled to survive, leaving him on his own a lot. Sol survived by his wits, and getting a spot in this program was nothing short of a miracle.

Phoenix noticed another wound on his calf that still looked red. A stitch had been left in, mistake number one, and the skin had puffed up around it in an attempt to rid itself of the foreign intruder. Sol wiggled his toes and noticed that the pain was less. *No more limping*, he thought. He didn't want anyone to get wind of any weakness.

Harken listened to them from the other side of the tree. He wanted to speak to them, but reaching out to others had somehow become almost impossible. He wasn't sure how it had happened or why, but silence had become what he did. It had been a full day now since he had spoken. The longest he had gone was 68 days without a word. He had worried about his interview for camp, but luckily, he found it easy to talk about his passion for chess. In his possession, he had a full set of chessmen minus two pawns and Bishop.

Time ticked by. Harken mulled over what he might say and then suddenly felt disgusted by his fear. He had to speak. Now. The next thing he knew, he stood facing Phoenix and Sol. Phoenix looked up and saw a boy who seemed sad when he smiled. Sol ran his fingers over the bumpy scar on his leg.

The reluctant smile spoke. "Hey," he said.

"Hey," Sol nodded. "Sit." He pointed to the ground next to him.

Harken obeyed and Phoenix opened her book to page 787. She ran her pointer finger down the page and stopped at a random place and read, *"kindle: verb, to start a fire, cause a flame; to spring up; to set fire to or ignite; to excite, stir up, get going, rouse; to light up, illuminate; The moon kindled the countryside.*"

"Come on, we'll never use that word," snickered Sol.

Harken actually liked words even though most of them remained locked away in his head. "Her words kindled hope," he blurted out. He immediately regretted the offering.

Phoenix smiled. "Good one." She shut the great whale of a book with a thump, sending dust motes flying. *Her words kindled hope,* she thought. Cool. She liked him and the boy with the scars.

High above them, Cedar realized she was holding her breath. She placed her hands on her racing heart and leaned back. A trail of black ants proceeded along a crevice in the bark beneath her foot, two worlds unaware of one another occupied the same space. Driven by a genetic code, the ants were headed for the leaves. Once there, they each would take a bite and then carry the piece home. She, on the other hand, would be in charge of her fate. Genetics had set her parameters only. Cedar closed her eyes.

Perhaps this girl with the white rat would teach her to read. Yes, this was surely the beginning of something very exciting. She could barely stop from leaping down in front of her, but some instinct told her to be patient.

Instead, Cedar gazed up and focused on the ever-present gray clouds that ebbed and flowed above her like the river that flowed around her. Here and there, light fell through, its beams full of whirling dust. The dust seemed to be less, but it still fell on most days. The book she felt would surely explain everything.

Chapter 6
Gauntlet

A monkey screamed, jolting Cedar out of her trance. The camp leader marched back into the courtyard. He had decided that perhaps he should say something although it didn't align with his mission statement which basically relied on the idea that less is more. He didn't intend on teaching them anything, he was just going to give them the opportunity to learn on their own by doing. All eyes were on him.

Cedar took this moment to scuttle down the tree. She was almost as good at it as the island monkeys. Just as her feet touched the ground, she turned to see the boy with the wormy black curls notice her. She froze. Blue eyes collided with brown or were they green? They changed with the light. The camp leader spoke, his voice harsh and impersonal. The boy turned away from her to listen, and Cedar took this opportunity to vanish.

"You are here because your parents or caretakers are free thinkers, people who still have hope for the future. This week will test your stamina. You have shelter and limited food. Your mission is to survive, and to produce a new idea or invention that will help secure a future for mankind."

He then turned and marched back into the building. The stone arch above the doorway read 1857. The small group of free thinkers stood in silence wondering what to do next.

Cedar raced down to the river path and grabbed her bike.

She thought about:

the music
the big book
was that a white rat?
reading
dust in her mouth
blue eyes
ring in her nose
the word *kindled*

She pedaled north, pumping hard. The bike strained beneath her. She stood again on her pedals and let the wind run its fingers under her shirt. The truth was that she wanted to meet them all, talk to them all and befriend them all. This was huge. How should she go about it? She had never made a friend. She decided she would have to make herself useful to them, so she gripped the rusted handlebar and willed herself to go faster. The wheels complained as they lurched over the uneven path. Cedar's fingers were covered in rings, every one, and it didn't stop there. Bracelets of all sorts adorned every inch of her arms and lower legs, but it wasn't decoration she desired. She was after protection, armor. She knew if she bled, she died.

She glistened, thought Harken. He usually tried to avoid eye contact, but it happened, and their gaze hung and intertwined until he had to turn and listen to this red-faced man. When the man exited, Harken turned back to the girl, but she was gone. Was she covered in bracelets? Had he really seen her? He wasn't sure.

Rattled by this vision, he turned back to the girl with the book and the friendly boy. The gauntlet had been thrown and campers were forming into small groups or heading off on their own. Sol indicated with a nod of his head that Harken should follow the girl with *Webster's unabridged Dictionary of the English Language* and him.

This was almost too good to believe as Harken had never been included in any circle. He actually smiled a little as they sauntered off: Sol ignoring the pain in his foot, Phoenix thinking about looking up the word *gauntlet* and Harken thinking about the girl from the tree.

Their base camp, the remains of a hospital, towered over a knoll at the tip of Roosevelt Island, which sits in the East River between what was Manhattan and Queens. As the post war years mounted, history faded. It was like starting over. This tiny island had gone through many metamorphoses. It was once home to all who were shunned by society. Hospitals and sanatoriums housed the poor and the sick, and now it was a home to a survival camp, the root of a dream, a dream about finding a way back to a future.

Chapter 7
Carnivore

Cedar saw the rodent before it saw her. It waggled through the sparse grass, nose gently drifting over the rocky ground. It was hungry, that was all. It didn't worry, ever. Instinct ran it through its paces day in and day out.

Cedar pulled her knife out as she rolled her bike to a stop. Her eyes opened wider; her breath slowed. She was on point like a wolf but so much more than a wolf. She had a brain that processed information at lightning speed.

In just seconds, she calculated the rodent's weight, imagined it on the spit, measured the distance between them, added in its speed, noted possible escape routes, and planned her attack. She thought about the big red book, the white rat, listened to a monkey move above her, noticed the wind picking up, and then she moved with the deliberate intent to kill. The animal sensed her and froze.

She leapt more like a dancer than a killer, but then can't dancers be killers? The victim ran toward her instead of away. What luck! She landed on it. It squirmed and lashed about, shrieking. Yellow teeth clattered on her bracelets. Her knife slid across its soft throat, and warm blood gushed into the outside world as if it was glad to be free of the body.

Now, the knife found the gut and sliced it open. Quickly, she eviscerated the organs and tossed the body into the bike basket.

Dinner, she thought as she trotted to the ever-present river to wash. Cedar didn't think about killing like her mother and grandmother had. She killed to eat and that was all. There was no thought of a trophy, rites of passage or a day of sport. Her mouth watered.

Garnal smiled when he spotted Cedar on her bike. The smile broadened when he saw the meal bouncing in the basket. She came gliding into the station like a warrior, her armor clinking and glowing in the muted light. Her hair was dark with sweat; a red smear of blood ran from the left corner of her lips to her ear. Garnal set right to work, stirring the fire pit that he kept smoldering most of the time. Cedar left the bounty for Garnal to prepare and headed off to find the Slack Man.

Sharing was an unspoken rule. Garnal, Cedar, and Slacker had no space to dream about a better future. Instead, they stumbled through the rubble of the past every day, but had little time to learn from it.

Meanwhile, not too far north of the fire pit, five feet under the rubble of fallen buildings, groundhogs stirred in the victim's burrow. It was dark and cool. The tunnel had five entrances which ran in all directions, totaling 43 feet in all. Instinct told them to sleep and they did. Overhead, the partially exposed skeleton of a Native American, a Lenape female, hung like a chandelier. She had died giving birth to her first child.

Chapter 8
Nascent

The Three Musketeers, as they might have been nicknamed if the world hadn't shifted and left them with little history or sense of what had come before, headed north along the river on the east side of the island. Phoenix spoke first, "It was a monkey that ran off with the music box."

Harken liked the sound of her voice. "Why would there be monkeys here?" His voice leapt out in spurts, unsure of itself.

"A good question, a very good question. What do we know about monkeys?" Sol retied what was left of a red bandana around his neck and danced in front of them with arms dangling, mouth in a wide grin.

They both laughed at his monkey antics. Harken's laugh was like a bark and Phoenix's a high shriek. "According to my dad," said Sol, "they live below the equator, so what are they doing this far north?"

"Maybe there was a circus here when the missiles landed." Harken had seen pictures of a circus in a book his dad had read to him.

"Remind me, what exactly is a circus?" asked Phoenix. She knew what missiles were and radiation and pollution but not a circus.

"It's a traveling show held under a tent. I think they had all kinds of animals trained to act like humans." Harken offered.

Sol shook his head. *Only man would laugh at animals taught to act in his image,* he thought.

Harken thought of a story he had heard about elephants learning to paint. Sadly, the last elephant had starved to death long before Harken was born. But monkeys were resilient and smart enough to adapt. Yet, the few on this tiny island were stranded because it was not in their nature to swim. The Three Musketeers would soon discover the rusted cages of the original island monkeys in the ruins of the Streckers Laboratory and put together the pieces of their origin puzzle.

Phoenix sat and opened her book, always her first step toward understanding. Sol and Harken joined her in what would become a ritual for them, and in a world lacking any, they hungered for it. Her neck curved quietly, suspending her head over the pages like a small sun, her yellow hair stuck out in every direction. She hunted down the word *circus* but was side tracked by *clairvoyant* and *City of Light*.

Words traveled between them, building something they needed, something they loved. Each syllable tightened their bond. They needed words to help them understand each other and to help them navigate their confusing world.

The more Phoenix read, the more they were humbled by the depth of a culture that knew so much. Yet, thought Harken, *that culture is gone.* Sol thought about the idea that perhaps man needed to start over every thousand years while Phoenix thought about how it made sense to sleep when it was dark. Three minds stimulated by the same words, each in different worlds of thought, sat across from one another.

A half a mile north of them, Garnal's fire reached its critical temperature for combustion and came to life. He walked around the pit five times and then veered off to locate what he needed to cook the rodent. These objects had no names. He just needed them. His friend who glittered had a name, Cedar, and she called him Garnal. He loved Cedar.

"I smell smoke." Sol scrambled to stand, his head drifting from side to side sniffing the air. "Let's check it out." He rubbed his right foot up and down his left calf trying to ease the pain. The book slammed shut, and they set out cautiously toward the smoke.

"Someone started it," whispered Phoenix.

"It could be another camper?" said Harken.

"Yeah, or the island monster!" Sol smiled.

The fire was easy to find, but they stayed back. Instinct told them to be careful. A man was tending a fire pit. Long arms swung from sloping shoulders. His dirty brown hair, wrestled into a tight knot, revealed large ears. He had a dark beard that touched his chest. Silently, the three newcomers came to the same conclusion that the stranger didn't seem like a threat.

As they stared at Garnal, Cedar crept up behind them. Harken hheard her bracelets tinkling against one another and slowly turned his head. He knew it was her, and she was glad it was him.

He touched the others, and they too turned. Cedar dropped to a squat to be on their level and wrapped her arms around her knees. Phoenix thought she looked like a bird. Sol spoke first. "Hello," was all he said.

"Hey, I'm Cedar. I live here." A tentative smile appeared. Names were exchanged, and then Cedar stood and motioned for them to follow her toward the fire. When Garnal saw the strangers, he made a fast retreat into his gas station/home and locked the door. "That's Garnal. He's just shy. The meat will bring him back out." Cedar proceeded to prepare the rodent for the spit, and soon it sizzled over the low flames. Mouths watered, stomachs growled, bowels rumbled. They sat around the fire and stared into the flames.

"I saw you this morning." Harken felt brave. The island was casting a spell on him, a good one. He could talk. In the chaos back on the mainland, he tried to be invisible. It was too loud, too unpredictable and exhausting. But here, it was different. He loved the soothing sound of the river. He felt there was room for him to think and to speak. He came by his propensity for silence honestly as he hailed from a long line of Norwegian fishermen who rarely spoke. The constant howl of the arctic wind made silence a way of life for them.

Feeling shy, Cedar kept her eyes on the fire.

She thought about:

what she could say to Harken
her hook hanging in the East River
the music
thinking in words

Sol's big smile
the red book in Phoenix's pack

Finally, she spoke. "It's a small island." She poked at the meat.

"How small?" Sol liked measurements. "It's longer than it is wide, that's for sure."

"Garnal says it's 100 paces, 100 times." The fire snapped and hissed at them. Cedar was programmed to evaluate safety so she studied the visitors. Were these strangers good people? Should she trust them? Her breath joined theirs, limbs overlapped, hands helped words, lips grew soft, the book opened, pages turned, hair twisted around fingers with blackened nail beds. Cedar took in their ragged clothes, the scarred shins, the patches sewn to their packs, the silver ring in Phoenix's nose. It was all so beautiful. She devoured the details of their trappings as the sunlight set them aglow. She wanted to know everything about these three. She hadn't known that she wanted anything, really, except food. Now, she was starving for friends. She decided to trust them.

The taller boy fiddled with a long black curl that divided his face, the boy who asked the question rolled back on his heels, and Phoenix looked up the word *measure* and read aloud.

As she read, Cedar thought about how the past measured everything, it named everything, and she wondered why. She thought about the animal in the fire pit. No one here knew its name. There were no names in its world. Man gave it one. Cedar liked to think about stuff like that. People need names, want names so that they can stand apart from the crowd. Animals have no such needs. They want to be part of a whole.

"What's it like across the river?" Cedar had spent her entire life imagining it. She divided the meat leaving enough for Garnal and Slacker. The three did not question the division, they were guests.

They chewed with enthusiasm. "It's a mess," Sol volunteered first, his lips shining with fat.

"No one's in charge." Harken hated disorder.

"People team up, they keep on the move." Phoenix licked her fingers. "It isn't safe anywhere."

Harken wiped his hands on his pants. "It's better here, less people. People ruin everything. How many are on your island?"

Before Cedar could answer, dusk sank between them like a stone turning their words into whispers. Answers would have to wait. Darkness insisted that they move on, and they did, but first they agreed to keep their meeting a secret and gather again the next day, soon after sunrise.

Chapter 9
Asylum

Garnal met her at his door, sure that she would come with the meat. The door cracked open, a dirty hand emerged, and dinner was delivered. The door clicked shut, and Cedar moved on to her home in the basement of the asylum ruin. She liked it in the basement. It was warmer down there in the winter and cooler in the summer. But first, she headed up to the tower to see Slacker with the meat cooling in her bag. His door was open, and the last shards of sunlight shot through the opening: sharp, clean and bright.

His favorite room was an octagon shape with huge windows facing in every direction. Most had shattered, and he had to retreat to drier ground when the weather demanded, but he spent much time there, reading and looking out over the river and island. He was seeing more birds, and a bird had to eat, so he was feeling more hopeful about the future of the planet.

Slacker loved going through the asylum files. That's where he got all his stories. Cedar didn't know it yet, but tonight she would hear a story about a man who came to the island in 1889. He had arrived in NYC from Italy two years before and worked in a hat factory. The lead used to make the wool hats drove him mad, and he had murdered two women in cold blood. The records said he thought they were wolves.

Cedar loved to hear these stories of patients being admitted to the hospital so many years ago, and Slacker loved to tell them. That night, he welcomed her and his meal with the crooked smile that Cedar adored. His smile and his left side hadn't worked very well for the last two years, but he got around.

Cedar wanted to tell him about the others, but something in her said to wait. Their tiny world was simple, and the sudden appearance of mainlanders would definitely upset Slacker. Just then, Cedar felt her right-side twist, a familiar pain. The bleeding would start soon. *Not again.* She looked up to see Slacker preparing to read to her. Ignoring the pain, she curled up in her favorite chair, and he began.

"William Wickford, admitted December 12,1889. D.O.B. unknown. Non communicative 5'6" male, Caucasian, 30 – 40 years of age wearing heavy wool pants tied at the waist with a twisted rag. His shoes are worn and without laces."

"What does that mean, without laces?"

"Laces are used to tighten a shoe." Shoes were scarce now and Slacker had resorted to taping all of them with duct tape.

"Like duct tape?"

"No, but both do the job."

A supply of duct tape remained under strict lock and key, guarded by Slacker. He read on. *"His shirt is coarse cotton, buttons missing. Although it is frigid tonight, he has no coat but rather a leather vest lined with wool. Both his right and left forearms are tattooed, left with an angel, and the right sported with the devil."*

"Tattooed, what is that?" Cedar uncurled and drew closer to Slacker. He had her in his spell. Most of what she learned came from questions that she had about these admittance descriptions written by nurses so many years ago.

"Tattoo is, was an art form. The artist injects ink just under the skin with a needle to create designs or messages."

"Hmm… weird but interesting."

"Weight 175, pulse 72, respirations 20. The patient appears lethargic and fell asleep in the chair. Patient taken to showers by orderly and will be admitted to Ward 3." Slacker shut the book with a snap.

"One more please," begged Cedar, but she knew it was no use. Slacker was finished for the evening. She stood, gave Slacker a quick hug and headed to her lair in the basement. Her room was long and narrow. A row of rectangular windows that hadn't been opened in years looked out on the river. Cedar yanked the top dresser drawer ajar and sorted through the clean rags she kept for the bleeding that would most likely begin while she slept. She slid one between her legs and tied each end to her belt. In seconds, she was under the ancient woolen blankets and falling asleep.

She thought about:

William Wickford
a tattoo shaped like an angel
Harken
blood
the ground hog's yellow teeth

Her bracelets jingled as she turned in bed. Wind maneuvered around the Asylum, pushing its way in between the cracks, but Cedar didn't hear it. She was dreaming. She was in the tree again above Harken, but this time she had wings.

Chapter 10
Hopeful

Day two came early, especially for Harken. He was up before the sun, dressed and already down the hall, tapping on Sol's door, #14. He leaned forward, his forehead touching the wood and listened. He heard Sol and moved on to #5. Phoenix's door opened just as he raised his fist.

"Let's get out of here before anyone else wakes up," she whispered. The three tiptoed down the hall. Once outside, they stopped to look across the river at the island of Manhattan. The once geometric shapes that punctured the horizon were now softer, muted by war. Rumor had it that the island was now home to the worst misfits. Those interested in reinventing society had moved inland away from the coasts. Just then, a fish broke the surface of the fast-moving river. All three of them thought about eating it.

Turning north, they headed down a worn path. Pieces of the old roadway now lay in rubble complicating their progress. Sol took a left and scrambled over the debris. Harken and Phoenix followed. Stomachs grumbled.

"First things, first," said Sol. "We need food." He settled down on his haunches and opened his pack. Harken noticed that a jagged scar parted his curly hair. "Here it is."

Sol held up a jar of what looked like grasshoppers. Insects had fared better than most since the war and had become the new protein. "Have one," he offered.

Phoenix peered into the jar. "How old are they?"

"Captured alive about six days ago. They are actually descendants of cicadas who slept through the war." Sol munched on one.

Harken held out his stash of coffee beans and they leapt for it. Phoenix fed a bean to her rat, which proved to be a mistake. She had no food to offer but entertained her new friends by reading about cicadas from her book. Soon, fueled by caffeine, they headed out to find Cedar.

Excited to see her new friends, Cedar was already at the meeting place with a small warm potato for each. She fiddled with her bracelets and checked her knife. Then she heard them. From afar, their voices sounded like the river jumping over stones. Soon, three silhouettes appeared on the horizon. One seemed to be shaking all over. This turned out to be Phoenix wrestling with her now hyperactive rat.

Cedar waved and shouted, "Hungry?"

"Always," responded Sol as he accepted her gift of a potato.

"Delicious!" Phoenix mumbled with her mouth full.

"Thanks!" Harken smiled.

As they chewed, Cedar remembered the blood and hoped it wouldn't interfere. She wondered if Phoenix also bled. They walked four abreast.

The sun rose as always and tried its best to make things right on planet Earth. The soil too was trying to make a comeback and sent forth green recruits here and there. Soon they arrived at a ruin of twisted steel bent in every direction.

Without a word, Cedar began to climb. She was like a spider with its long sinewy limbs moving fluidly over the steel, feeling her way.

They followed. Sol jumped in first, then Phoenix and ending with Harken who hesitated for a moment. He was nervous but kept it to himself. Finally, he took a deep breath and began his ascent. *Don't look down, don't look down,* he repeated to himself. Just as he was about to say he was at the end of his abilities, Cedar slid onto what was once a part of the former roadbed. The perch was about ten feet square with a barrier on just one side. She pushed up against it and sat with her legs outstretched. The wind seemed stronger up here, dangerous even. The top of Sol's head appeared and then his smile. "This is nuts!" He scooted over by Cedar and surveyed the scene.

Next, Phoenix appeared, her mouth set in a straight line and finally, Harken. They sat shoulder to shoulder in silence, enamored by the height and view.

Cedar thought about:

the wind
Sol's shoulder pushing against hers
the pain in her side
Garnal's collection

Phoenix broke the silence, "What was this, a bridge?"
"Yeah, Roosevelt Bridge."
Phoenix smiled and retrieved her book. Pages rustled. All leaned toward the words. Breathing slowed, heart rates too, minds focused.

Phoenix read, "*Roosevelt Bridge opened to traffic in 1955. The 2,877-foot-long bridge crosses the East Channel of the East river at 40 feet over mean high water. When the 418-foot-long, 1000-ton vertical lift span is raised between the bridge's 170-foot-tall towers, a 100-foot clearance is provided for ships.*"

The wind wove its way between them. Sol held his face up to the sun and reconstructed the ruin into a bridge. Harken kept his head down, unable to really look around. If he did look, it felt unsafe as if he might jump. He felt certain that mankind belonged on the ground, and his insistence to go where he didn't belong was part of the problem that set the world on its course toward complete destruction. Sol interrupted his thoughts. "Shit, somebody is just below us."

Three heads leaned over the edge and looked down the fifty or so feet. It was Garnal. He lumbered along mumbling what sounded like a song. "It's Garnal. He won't see us; he hates to look up. His eyes are always downcast, searching for treasure. He collects stuff that's shiny or red. He loves red."

"He must like you," Sol offered. "You're shiny."

Cedar stared straight ahead and smiled. Phoenix closed the book and Harken cleared his throat. He had had enough of heights and wanted to start down, but he would have to lead out.

Below them, Garnal meandered along, arms swinging. Suddenly, the singing stopped, and he leaned over. "He's found something." Again, all looked over the edge of the platform except for Harken who decided to use this as a reason to take action. He turned onto his stomach and slid his legs over the edge searching for a foothold. He held his breath until his right foot found purchase and then proceeded to lower himself over the edge, swearing that he would never climb this again. All he could think about was getting down. Sweat curled the edges of his hair and trickled down his back. He wondered if he was a coward. He thought about fear a lot. Could it be used in a good way? Without it, could we survive?

He heard his friends clattering down above him and felt jealous of their bravery. What good did it do, to be frightened? Regardless, Harken felt his confidence resurge when his foot touched the ground. If he had known about Greek mythology, he might have compared himself to the son of Mother Earth, Antaeus, who was only powerful when grounded.

Garnal turned and saw the relief in Harken's face. To the islander, Harken seemed friendly. Garnal lowered his gaze and held very still, his fingers tightly curled around his newly found treasure. He hummed quietly and rocked back and forth. He could sense Cedar dangling above him. Harken nodded and smiled again, stepping back a bit, instinctively putting some space between them.

"Don't scare him off with that ugly face of yours. Say something," shouted Sol.

"My name's Harken."

"Brilliant," chuckled Sol.

Garnal shuffled his feet and continued to stare at the ground. Harken looked down too and noticed that his new friend was barefoot. Sol made landfall, followed quickly by the others. Garnal's humming grew louder.

Cedar stepped toward him and pointed at his hand. He raised his arm and uncurled his fingers. Resting on his flat meaty palm was what remained of a man's watch, circa 1960's. They all stared. There were numbers on one side. Phoenix remembered seeing one in her book. "It tells time."

"Cool, can I hold it?" asked Sol. Garnal's fingers closed over the treasure.

"That's a no, buddy." Harken snickered.

"I would love to take that apart," said Sol.

"That's not going to happen. It's Garnal's now and if he likes it, he won't give it up. He has others though."

"Really, where?'

Blood trickled down Cedar's inner thigh. She adjusted her legs trying to stop what was inevitable. Now, red traveled down her lower leg and around her right ankle. *Darn it,* she thought.

Phoenix noticed but said nothing about it. Hoping to give Cedar cover, she turned to her mates. "Let's go. We need to check in at school and see what's going on. Cedar, should we meet tomorrow?"

"Sure, meet me at the fire pit first thing." She smiled a 'thank you 'to Phoenix.

Chapter 11
Dubious

The three island newcomers headed south to the old Smallpox hospital. "Is it weird that we haven't seen any other campers?" Sol trotted backward to face them.

"Super weird."

"Nuts."

"Strange."

"Who cares!"

Laughter erupted from all as they made their way home trying to come up with words for weird.

"Creepy."

"Unusual."

"Our camp director!"

"Yeah, he's totally bonkers."

"Bonkers works."

Soon, they discovered the reason why they had seen no one. The ruin was deserted, and the boat was gone. Frantically, the three left behind searched the site but found no signs of what had happened. Had they been forgotten? Was this part of the challenge? Phoenix thought it was fine with her, she was happy with her team of four. "This could be part of the challenge," she offered.

"It's nuts if you ask me." Sol spun toward her. "Why would they leave us?"

"It's batty, that's what it is; what the hell?" Harken's voice cracked.

"But guys, it makes everything simpler. We don't have to deal with any of the others. I like our small team. We can survive now that we have Cedar." Phoenix sat and pulled out her book. Sol and Harken joined her; the circle grew tighter until their knees touched. Phoenix opened the book to a random page and read: "*Earth – the planet that we live on; the terrestrial globe: it is the fifth largest planet of the solar system and the third in distance from the sun; diameter 12,760 kilometers or 7,930 miles; period of revolution – one earth year; period of rotation – 24 hours; one satellite – the moon.*" As she read, the three-man circle settled down and seemed to breathe as one.

"So, if this island is a mile long," Sol thought out loud, "then earth's diameter is about 8000 island lengths." He absentmindedly scratched a scab on his arm.

Phoenix shut the book. She was immersed in thoughts of the earth spinning as it went around the sun. Sol thought about the delicious potato he'd just eaten, while Harken thought about planting his coffee beans. All three were aware that there was no one here to care for them. Self-doubt nibbled at the edges of their consciousness, but this was a resourceful trio and soon, they were emptying their packs of all that was edible and gathering wood for a fire in the yard.

Darkness was on its way and with it came uncertainty. Sol knelt and blew on the tiny flame. Harken and Phoenix sat watching the fire come to life. Their world grew even smaller as the darkness hemmed them in.

Harken thought about:

Cedar
the blood – he'd seen it
the watch
his mother
his fear of heights

Sol thought about:

the gas pumps – was there gas?
hunting groundhogs
the monkeys
catching a fish

Phoenix thought about:

Cedar's blood
finding parts for a bike
should they sleep in one room
feeding Ratty

They sat, each in his or her private world, while about a mile north of them, another fire burst to life as Cedar and Garnal cooked some more potatoes. Cedar felt excited about the change presented by the existence of the others.

Garnal did not think about the others at all. He fiddled with his new watch and thought about the other discovery he had made today. It was something big, something huge. He couldn't wait to show it to Cedar and Slacker. He didn't know it yet, but it would change everything.

Cedar left him at the fire and returned to Slacker with a few warm potatoes. First, she went downstairs to her room to replace the bloody cloth and then flew up the tower steps three at a time.

Slacker sat with his feet up on what was once the hospital director's desk, reading. "Listen to this: *Nellie Brown admitted on September 25, 1887. Diagnosis: undoubtedly insane and suffering from amnesia. Admitted from Belleview Hospital where she was taken by her landlord who said she was acting strangely. She had attracted attention in the emergency room and an article ran in the New York Times entitled, 'Who is this Insane Girl?' At this time, the patient is cooperative but irrational, stating that she is from Cuba. She is assigned to Ward 6.*" Slacker paused to eat his potato.

"Keep reading!" Cedar sat on his desk watching her father-figure chew his treat. Slacker was lucky as his teeth had held up pretty well, but he chewed slowly just to tease Cedar.

"Hang on." He wiped his mouth on his shirt and continued. "I will skip to her discharge note. *Patient, Nellie Brown, discharged on November 5th to a Peter Hendricks, a lawyer who claims that friends have agreed to care for the patient.*"

"So, what is so interesting about her story?"

"Here, a note is attached stating that Nellie Brown is none other than Nellie Bly, a journalist posing as a patient to spy on the asylum. Her article was printed in the paper exposing the institution, claiming that the patients here were horribly mistreated."

"I wonder what they did to them."

Just then, Slacker pulled a tattered black and white photograph out of the book, and they both leaned over and studied it. Women, two by two, walked on what looked like what was once called a lawn. All wore plain white dresses with long sleeves and white hats. Around each waist was a belt, from which dangled a thick rope that ran between patients and ended tied to some kind of cart. One woman's head was turned, another leaned over to pick something up. Behind the cart was what seemed to be the nurse in charge. She wore a pointed cap and leaned on the cart.

"Wow, it looks like a prison. They are tied together."

"It does seem like a prison, and it still is for us, sort of." Slacker sighed. Sometimes images of 'before 'rose up in him: his father kneeling in the garden, a pile of red tomatoes at his knees; his mother flying out the back door calling for him, the door catching her yellow skirt. The sky was blue, and the grass grew green and thick. He shook off the images and returned his attention to Cedar. "Now what have you been up to?"

Now it was her turn to tell a story, and she had a big one for him. As was her way, she didn't plan what she would say. She just blurted it out. "Others have arrived on the island." She watched him closely. He sat up, rigid.

"There are fifteen young people, male and female and one older man." She decided to keep it short and not overwhelm him. He stared at her and sat up straight.

"Where? Have you made contact?"

"I met three, a girl and two boys around my age, I think. They have met Garnal too. They are camped out on the southern tip and are starting some kind of camp."

Slacker stood up abruptly and did a lap around the octagon shaped room. "It had to happen. The river is narrow. But why here?" He did not expect an answer nor did Cedar proffer one. A stormy silence raged about them.

"One boy, Harken, is quiet. Phoenix, the girl, has a cool book and Sol is funny. I like them."

"I am going to check it out. Come with me." Slacker took charge and Cedar followed.

Back at camp, the three left behind were still a bit shaken by the sudden exodus and remained close to the fire, unwilling to separate just yet. Sol toyed with the edge of a thick scab on his leg. Its black edges could be lifted but the center held tight. He was dying to rip it off but knew better. After a long while, Phoenix stood indicating that she would head to bed. "Let's sleep on it," she tossed over her shoulder. Sol followed.

Harken remained at the fire. The moon rose in the sky. Stars blinked on and off. He thought he might feel happy, a new feeling for him. He felt safer now with friends. The flame had him in its spell, and he stared as if in a trance.

Nearby, the Roosevelt Island monkeys messed about in the laboratory ruin as they settled in for the night. Ironically, they slept in the lab where scientists experimented on their ancestors to discover how the brain functioned. Now, it was just home to them. The island ground hog population snuggled into their den too, and the Lenape skeleton hung above them as always.

Slacker and Cedar's walk to meet the newcomers was a silent one. They slowed their pace as they approached the ruin, and then stood in the shadows watching Harken. Slacker thought, "If he stays at the fire for a count of 50, then this will all work out." Magical thinking was something Slacker did for his own entertainment. He stared at Harken's gently curving shoulders. Cedar too watched her new friend.

Meanwhile, Harken felt their presence. It prickled around him. He stood suddenly and turned to face them. Both parties stared. Moonlight fell between them. Both men, one old and one young, longed for a weapon.

Am I safe? they both wondered. *Is he a threat?* Cedar smiled and took Slacker's rough hand in hers to reassure him that he was safe.

Harken struggled to speak. "Cedar," he managed to get out.

"Harken, this is Slacker. He lives up in the tower on the other end of the island. I live there too. He's super smart and kinda like a dad to me." She shuffled toward the fire, pulling Slacker along. She glittered in the moonlight. Harken felt his shoulders relax. This was not an enemy.

Slacker took a breath and noticed a tightening in his chest. It was a feeling. *One should feel a feeling*, he thought and this one was for Cedar. He felt a need to protect her and guide her. Could he share her?

Cedar tugged on his hand, and he followed her lead and sat. The fire snapped and barked, sending small missiles of light into the dark. Inside the ruin, two hearts slowed as each gave in to sleep.

The three around the fire stared into the flames. Slacker broke the silence, "Why are you here on the island?" He drove a stick into the fire.

Harken turned toward him and surprised himself with three complete sentences. "My parents actually signed me up for this experimental camp. I think they were just tired of trying to keep me alive. Needed a break. So here I am."

"So where are the other campers?" Slacker was confused. Harken explained what he knew. Soon, the words flowed and connected them. They grew easy with each other around the warm fire. The three spoke in hushed tones, Slacker milking stories about what life was like across the river from this young stranger. Could he, Slacker, be coaxed off island? He didn't think so but for Cedar, her world was opening up. Perhaps he should make an effort to go off island with her and explore. The arrival of these campers was a sign that they couldn't hide away from reality forever.

Chapter 12
Discovery

The next day, Garnal was up early. He wanted to get back to the discovery he made yesterday, so he hurried through his morning routine. First, he checked to see if the Mercury's door was closed, then he opened and shut it a second time to be sure. Next, he grabbed the keys and opened the main door, stepping out into his day. Once this door was locked and checked, he touched the gas pumps. Satisfied, he headed toward the northern tip of the island where the Blackwell Island lighthouse lay in ruin. It was just a pile of rubble embedded with the huge Fresnel lens which once warned ships of the river's tricky currents. To Garnal, it looked like a huge eye. Excited, he scrambled around the lighthouse debris and picked his way down a steep embankment to his discovery, a cave.

The entrance was as tall as he was and about twice as wide. He stepped into the quiet darkness. Garnal had no fear of the dark as he didn't have the imagination that created fantasies, good or bad. Water dripped steadily. At about twenty or so steps in, he arrived at the hidden treasure, a majestic canoe marooned up on a ledge. Today, Garnal noticed the red and black drawings softened by time that decorated both sides. He touched the rim and ran his hand along it, fingers tingling. He thought he heard bells ringing. Pulling himself up on the ledge, he looked down into the boat. Lying in the bottom was a strange contraption that looked like an animal trap. Garnal had no idea what it was. Strewn here and there were small pointed stones. He twirled one in his hand, the tip was sharp. He stuffed it in his pocket and then took another. Eager to share what he found, he set off to find Slacker and Cedar.

An hour later, Garnal had not just Cedar and Slacker but a line of five eager explorers following him. A man of few words, he didn't try to explain his discovery.

"He's never been this excited about anything really. I wonder what it is." Cedar put her hand on Garnal's shoulder.

"A skeleton?"

"A bomb?"

"A pile of cheeseburgers?"

"Please be food."

The guesses went on and on until they saw the mouth of the cave, and then all fell silent and stared as if they stood before a mystical shrine. Garnal entered the cave first with his entourage on his heels.

As they crossed from light into darkness, the fight or flight reaction sent their hearts racing, dilated their pupils, and tightened their muscles as the brain released cortisol. A dim light made its way through a crack in the ceiling of the cave lighting the treasure waiting for them on the ledge.

A small line of six stood taking it in. Cedar reached out first and touched the red shape that looked like a turtle painted on the bow. And as if she had hit the 'on 'button, the cave exploded with discussion. Everyone was talking at once.

"Who can swim?"

"Is it safe?"

"Are there paddles?"

"Yes, look, there they are."

"Should we give it a go?"

"What kind of boat is this?"

"I wonder how old it is?"

With Sol leading the charge, they had the boat in the water in no time. No one had been in a canoe except Slacker who showed them how to use the oars and steer the little ship.

"Come on, we can do this!" shouted Sol. "We won't go far." Slacker's eyebrows rose up and touched. Garnal smiled and waved.

"Don't worry, it'll be fun." Cedar pushed her dirty brown hair back out of her eyes. Harken noticed a red mark above her right eye shaped like a crescent moon.

Chapter 13
Peregrination

Sol held the end of the canoe steady. Its nose bobbed in the current as if eager to be on its way. Cedar brushed her fingertips along the worn rim. They tingled and a smile arrived unannounced. She looked back at Phoenix and Harken who seemed blurry around the edges.

She thought about:

Slacker
the dictionary
her new ring
the red turtle
Garnal's smile

Harken hopped in next and then Phoenix. Cedar grabbed an oar and looked straight ahead. Phoenix touched her rat, Sol gave a push and leapt into the stern. The four fit nicely in the long boat. It slid out into the river, happy to be where it belonged. Cedar and Sol were awkward at first but soon fell into a rhythm. Everyone but Sol was nervous. What if they capsized? Swimming was not a skill that they had time to develop in this post-apocalypse world. The novice sailors were silent and on high alert.

Their silence was soon interrupted by a slight ringing in their ears. The air felt cooler. Goosebumps appeared up and down arms and legs. Cedar drew the paddle up into her lap and Sol did the same. Now the current was steering the boat. Cedar pointed up to the sky. It was blue.

"Is that a bird?" whispered Phoenix. Birds shot across the now brilliantly blue sky dividing it into an infinite number of shapes. The air filled with calls, a madhouse of notes.

Sol looked back at the island and shouted, "Look guys – trees!" Incredibly tall trees, thick with green leaves and strung with long twisting vines, now lined the shore. Small explosions of color went off everywhere.

The four stared, the boat drifted. Cedar pointed, and her friends followed the trajectory of her finger to see a tall brown creature step out from the tree line and make its way down the muddy bank on four spindly legs. Its ears twitched like tiny wings. Huge black eyes surveyed the scene, and then it dropped its delicate nose into the river. Phoenix grabbed her dictionary and opened it to the 'D's.

"I've seen a picture of this, it's a deer, I think." The pages flipped. "There it is." She read aloud, "*wild animal: any of a family of hoofed, cud-chewing animals as the moose, reindeer, caribou, etc. The males usually bear antlers that are shed annually.*"

Eight hands pulled at the book to see better, but when they looked up, the deer was gone. So intent on identifying the species, they missed experiencing it. All stared at the spot where it stood, trying to will it back. The symphony around them seemed almost deafening. Then above it all, a high-pitched wail pierced the din.

"What's that?" Cedar held her hand up. Sol dug his oar into the current and turned the canoe toward the sound. The wailing waxed and waned. It was sharp and lean.

"It sounds human," whispered Phoenix. Cedar rowed hard to shore.

She thought about:

the deer's eyes
the color green
a tattoo of an angel
dreams
why did this sound hurt her heart?

Together, they managed to get the canoe pulled up on shore. Then they stood listening for the cry. The wind was flooded with noises, but the human wail wound its way through all of it. It drove them, it propelled them to it.

Cedar went first, pushing the foliage aside, her fingers reading the surfaces of the plants. Smooth, prickly, soft, sticky. She did not know how to think about what had happened, she just wanted to stop the crying. She stumbled upon a worn path that twisted up a steep embankment. Halfway up, the wail turned to a whimper. They hurried.

Cedar could smell blood, and then she was there with her friends just behind her. The four stood motionless staring at a scene that was both horrific and beautiful like a delightful nightmare. There on the ground lay a young indigenous woman with her newborn infant on her chest.

Phoenix moved first. She knelt down beside the woman who looked so peaceful. Her delicate hands held her newborn child. The infant shuttered, and his mother's hands fell away. His ruddy skin was covered in blood, his dark black hair swirled in matted ringlets. Ever so gently, Phoenix turned the baby toward her and picked him up. Cooing softly to him, she covered him with her shirt. His umbilical cord dangled precariously. He snuffled and whimpered. Sol leaned in for a better look and gently tucked the cord into Phoenix's shirt. As they fussed over the baby, Harken stared at the mother. Just then, her arms slipped down and lay at her side. The motion startled him. The ground between her legs was soaked in blood. She wore a leather shirt beaded around the edges and a skirt now black with blood. Her face was so still, a thin scar divided her forehead.

He knelt and touched her cheek. It was still warm, but she was gone. No heart beat, no lungs filled with air. He felt like he was standing inside a miracle where life and death happen at the very same moment. A door opens between the two worlds, and one exits just as the other slips in. They cross paths but do not meet. Cedar put her hand on Harken's shoulder. It prickled. He stood. Still, no one had spoken.

A creature rustled in the dense thickets, a bird shrieked, leaves swiveled on their stems, branches complained, clouds changed shape. The dead woman lay in the heart of all things living.

"I'm a blank right now, it's crazy. I can't think," Sol spoke first.

"I think we stumbled through a time portal, if that's possible," Harken mumbled. "It's not, is it?"

The baby rooted looking for its mother and nourishment. Phoenix arranged her shirt so the baby lay against her skin. He was warm and sticky. The tiny marvel squirmed a bit, and her eyes filled with tears.

"Damn good timing for him," said Sol.

Harken lifted his eyes to Cedar's. "But not for the mother. What are you thinking, Cedar?"

Cedar shook her head and crossed her silver arms. "I'm trying to believe what I see? Are we dreaming this all up? How could we have stepped back in time? Can we get back?"

Phoenix rocked back and forth, soothing the baby. "I'm thinking she is Native American for sure. Do you guys think we were somehow sent here to save the baby?"

"We are where? We are when?" Sol asked. He touched the baby's head.

"The questions will have to wait because this baby needs to eat." They all happily focused on a concrete problem. They would need to find the mother's family, and so they headed up the steep slope.

Phoenix went first with all supporting her. When they reached level land, they gazed out over an island now teaming with life. A huge flock of birds swooped overhead. Tall green grasses topped with golden tassels reached their waists. Trees towered all around them, their leafy branches reaching out to one another. There were no buildings, no roads, no signs of their old life anywhere.

A cry rang out, and they all jumped. It was the baby reminding them to keep moving. Phoenix touched his soft rosy lips, and he suckled her finger. Cedar pointed to a path.

"So we are just going to walk until we find his people. What if they aren't happy to see us?" Sol itched at his latest scab. Ratty appeared and sniffed the tiny new soul's head.

Phoenix indicated that Harken should take the dictionary from her pack. "Look up Native American. I know I have read about them before." They sat in their familiar circle with their talisman in the center. Pages turned. The ritual made them all feel better.

Harken read aloud, *"Native Americans also known as the American Indian are the indigenous people who inhabited the Americas before the Europeans arrived. There are 574 recognized tribes within the US. Their ancestors arrived in what is now the United States at least 15.000 years ago from Asia via Beringa."*

He snapped the big book shut and looked up. "There is so much to learn. How did we ever get from this paradise to that mess we just left?" Void of answers, everyone just nodded and grunted. The four novice explorers from the future faced the age-old problem that has aggravated man forever. He likes answers not mysteries.

Cedar looked at the sun. "It's halfway through the day according to the sun. Let's get going." She stood and they followed. Sol raced ahead, leaping every now and then and shouting back sightings. He pointed to a great patch of yellow flowers standing six feet tall. Soon, they reached a forest. The entourage paused. Massive tree trunks rose up like an army. Their roots crisscrossed the forest floor curling and coiling into fantastical shapes. Deep green moss adorned the maze.

The village of trees rustled and vibrated with life. Each one was like a castle with turrets bursting through the canopy to find the sunlight. *If this is a dream,* thought Cedar, *I hope I never wake.* The small line of now five, made its way. The baby slept. It was cooler and darker in the woods.

Suddenly, Sol's hand flew up. They had come upon what they would later learn was an elk. The procession halted as the beast raised its regal head to stare at them. It stood six feet tall at the shoulder. Its antlers were four feet across and two feet tall at least. Unconcerned with their presence, it snorted softly and proceeded to munch on some tree bark. A gray bird fluttered down and roosted on an antler, then another until there were three.

They chittered and ruffled their feathers. It seemed that the great beast and the tiny passengers were seasoned travel companions. Harken thought about the huge beast wandering through the forest with its singing chandelier upon its head.

Sol waved them on, and the four interlopers delicately proceeded past the musical marvel giving it plenty of room. Dirty hands reached out to touch rough bark and soft pine needles. Carefully, they pulled long stems covered in prickers aside. When the breeze picked up, the trees swayed and jabbered. They traveled within a symphony that suddenly had a new voice join in. "Drums," said Phoenix. The sound fired off a synapse in Sol's brain triggering a fear response. He crouched lower, slowed his pace and scanned the landscape. All senses were hyper aware.

"The baby should protect us," whispered Harken.

Phoenix looked down at the tiny creature curled at her breast. *So young to be a hero,* she thought.

Nearby, the child's tribe, the Lenape, had gathered around a fire pit. They were worried about Katami who was heavy with child. She had gone off to collect berries and should have returned by now. The men beat out a soothing rhythm that told the story of the impending birth. If the four interlopers had been Lenape, they would have understood the drums' message. The forest thinned as the drums grew louder, and the line of young people from the future walked a path hewn hundreds of years before toward the sound.

Again, Sol's hand flew up. They paused at the edge of a clearing and watched the tribe. Tall figures shuffled around a small fire, spinning at times with arms out, fingers reaching. Great long tangles of dark hair drifted behind them.

The baby whimpered. Phoenix looked down at his tiny face. "It's time to meet your family little one." She raised him high above her head and stepped into sight. Sol held his breath, Cedar pulled at her shirt, and Harken stretched to his full height.

The drums fell silent. The circle grew still. Harken felt like he was standing in a sea of grass. The moment stretched on. The sea moved in waves around the interlopers. Two worlds separated by four hundred years gazed upon each other for one long minute and then another until suddenly, the silence was shattered by the child's wail.

Warm blood ran down Phoenix's arm. She lowered the tiny boy to her chest and then held him out toward the circle. Sol moved to her side as did Harken, and Phoenix felt their shoulders push against hers. *Thank you,* she thought. Cedar moved forward two steps.

The dancers froze, the drummers stopped. A cacophony of voices filled the air, and then an older female raced past them toward the mother. A tall man strode toward them, his hands floated over the tasseled grass. His long hair entwined with white feathers hung to his waist. He was flanked by two women with skirts billowing in the wind. The sun bore down. The grass swirled around them. The infant squirmed in her hands. And then they were upon them, standing in silence, staring.

At close range, the three were magnificent in beaded leather. The women had black hair braided into tight rows with gray and red feathers dangling. The man's leathery face was rich with lines and wisdom.

Phoenix spoke. "Your baby," she said as she handed the innocent over. The tall man accepted the child and wrapped him in a rough blanket. He spoke. His voice was deep and soft like distant thunder. The women came closer and cooed over the baby. More ran past them toward the river.

Time seemed to stand still as the young ambassadors from the future stood in the presence of those from the past. The universe quivered. What happens when two worlds collide? What happens when there is no shared language or history?

Harken thought about just that. He twirled the tiny bag of coffee beans in his pocket. Cedar took one step closer and cooed over the baby along with the women. Sol tried to hold still and Phoenix wept softly.

Cedar spoke. "We heard your baby crying and followed the sound. We are so sorry that his mother," she looked back at her new friends and continued, "is dead."

As she spoke, Sol tried to convey the message with hand and body movements. The tall man watched intently trying to understand. He almost smiled. Sol had found a way to connect.

Just then, wailing cries from the search party could be heard. They had found her. The tall man looked up, his smile retreated. Two women, both older with long gray hair pulled back into braids, took the baby from his frozen stance and headed toward the fire pit just as the impromptu funeral procession emerged from the dark woods into the bright clearing. A large man carried the mother in his arms. He stared straight ahead. The others trailed behind him, crying and moaning. As they passed, the tall man who had spoken turned and followed them until they all disappeared into the trees.

The four stood in the tall grass like statues unsure of what to do or what to even say to each other. Wailing cries from the mourners faded as the procession made its way deeper into the forest. Phoenix sat and pulled out the book. The others joined her sitting in their usual circle with legs crossed and heads bowed over the open pages.

She read: *"Time Travel – moving between different points in time. Not all scientists think that time travel is possible but some do. General relativity provides scenarios that could allow travelers to go back in time because time slows down or speeds up depending on how fast you move relative to something else. Approaching the speed of light, a person inside a spaceship would age much slower than his twin at home. Einstein's theory of ..."* her voice trailed off.

"I'm hearing the words but I don't get it," Sol pulled the book toward him. All heads nodded.

"We are so in the dark here," croaked Harken.

"Yeah, and it's actually going to be dark soon. Listen, I know this sounds crazy, but I think I want to go back or try to go back. I can't just leave Slacker and Garnal without letting them know what happened. Then we could come back with them, or should we just stay?" Cedar looked over her shoulder through the lush trees at the sun now painting the sky orange and pink.

Harken pulled at the long grass. "We would be crazy not to stay here. I mean compare this to what we have back in the future."

"That sounds weird, 'back in the future,'" Cedar said it again, "Back in the future."

"Well, I'm in one hundred percent, one thousand percent!" Sol did a backward somersault out of the circle and stood. He whirled around with arms out. "It's amazing, amazing!"

Phoenix slammed the big book shut with a thump, it was a sound she loved. "Let's do it!" Just then, her tiny passenger made an appearance. A pink nose and two black eyes peered out of her pack. Even Ratty had made the trip through time. She stood and reached out to her small tribe of four. "Let's go back to the future for Slacker and Garnal, but first we should leave them a gift – don't you think?"

"Maybe one or two of us should stay put?" Sol wanted to stay.

"I think we should stick together." Cedar did not want to lose these new friends.

"Together is better for me," said Harken. He too did not want to lose his first friends.

In the end, they left three of Cedar's bracelets, and two ancient playing cards circa 2000 that Phoenix had found on the mainland. On one side of the card was a map and on the other, two-headed figures dressed in red, blue and yellow held swords and stared off into space.

Meanwhile, the setting sun and distant drum beat encouraged them to hurry, and so they set off retracing their steps through the forest toward the river, toward the future or would it be their past? Soon, they were in the canoe and paddling back the way they had come. All were silent. The paddles dipped, and the river slapped the sides of their small ship. Questions spun in their heads. Would they make it back? Would it be in the exact same spot in time? Was this a mistake? Could they get back to paradise?

The ringing in their ears returned. The air grew cold, the sky gray, and the island was once again a pile of rocks and scrubby weeds. Sol leaned back as he turned the nose of the longboat toward the cave. It was low tide, so the boat maneuvered easily into its old home, and the four lifted it up onto the ledge. Quickly, they exited the cave. Absorbed in their thoughts, they trudged along in a single file behind Cedar toward Garnal's fire pit.

Harken stared at the back of Cedar's head and thought about an orange butterfly that had landed on his arm. Phoenix adjusted her back pack and thought about the baby's tiny mouth around her finger. Sol thought about the tall man's beautiful voice. Cedar thought about what to say to Slacker.

Chapter 14
Adjudicate

As night arrived, two very different groups sat around a very similar fire not far from each other but 400 years apart. Both discussed the other. Both had big decisions to make. The Lenape spoke of spirits and omens as the baby's father paced around the circle, soothing his tiny offspring. Smoke mingled with the debate. The tall man, who was their chief, made it clear that they should be open to accepting strangers. He had found the gifts, which now made their way around the circle. Two of the bracelets glistened on his wrist. Young and old examined the playing cards with awe. Then, as was the custom, each made a tribute to the mother, now a spirit who would linger among them for eleven days. Several women prepared the body for burial.

Nearby, the four time-travelers sat around their fire still mute. The situation was so big, so unexpected, so amazing, and so hard to believe that they didn't know where to begin.

Phoenix pulled out her book, and the pages furled open. She turned them carefully until she found what she hunted and then read: "*Manhattan-Colonial era: The area that is now Manhattan was long inhabited by the Lenape Native Americans, until it was first mapped and explored by Henry*

Hudson in 1609." She looked up at the others. "Lenape," she repeated.

"Lenape, cool. I like the sound of it." Sol smiled.

"Lenape," whispered Cedar.

"So, since we saw no signs of any people who look like us, we must have landed before this Henry Hudson. It must be pre 1609. That's insane," Harken concluded.

"If we do go back, how do we know that we will arrive at the same moment in time?" Cedar worried. She scratched at her arm with the missing bracelets.

"A gamble, but a good one I think," said Sol. He wanted to return no matter what.

"I'm scared, but I think we should go. What have we got to lose?" Harken twirled a stick in the dirt. He suddenly knew he was going back.

White pages turned in the firelight as Phoenix searched for clarity. Just then, she remembered Ratty and pulled him from the bag. He made a bee line for her shirt pocket and safety. His tiny head popped out, and he surveyed the scene. Phoenix rubbed his ear. "Let's do it. I'm in." She stuffed the big book back into its pack and stood. Ratty disappeared into her shirt pocket now stained with blood.

The circle debated. Cedar's bracelets rattled as she spoke. "I want to invite Slacker and Garnal. Is that okay?"

Harken turned to her, "I bet it will be hard for Garnal to go, but sure, we should definitely ask. Do we all agree?"

'Yes 'went around the circle. Plans were made to return to the fire pit when the sun was directly overhead the next day. Cedar thought they should take off at about the same time as they did today. Phoenix suggested each bring a gift for the Lenape people.

"Yeah, I'll raid the hospital lab and see what they have," said Sol.

Harken turned toward Sol. "I'll go with!"

Cedar thought of all the books in the hospital library or maybe she could find something cool from Slacker's secret stash. The wind picked up blowing the smoke in every direction. The four stood, anxious to get going. Tomorrow couldn't come soon enough. Things could change, the portal could close.

"'To sleep, to sleep, perchance to dream,' Slacker loves to say that." Cedar split from the circle and headed to check on Garnal and then home to deal with Slacker. She wondered what he would do, how he would react.

On the way back to hospital, the three discussed what they would bring. The island monkeys gathered in the trees as they approached the ruin which gave Sol an idea. What if they brought a monkey as a gift? As he crawled into his cot in number 22, his mind whirled with ways to trap a monkey. Phoenix was too tired to think and Harken thought about Cedar.

Chapter 15
Galvanize

Back at the tower, Cedar approached Slacker with a rip in her heart. She felt sure that he would choose to stay put. He was asleep in his favorite chair, hands folded and feet up on his desk as she approached him. Cedar studied him closely. With his head thrown back, his face had relaxed, and he looked much younger than his seventy or so years. She thought about him as a child and as a young man living in the world when it was normal or at least pre-disaster.

Suddenly, she felt guilty that she knew so little about him. She wished she had asked questions about his life before the disaster. He was just thirty when the lights went out. Cedar had only thought of him in relation to her, her support system.

Coarse gray curls sprouted here and there on his head like a weedy garden. She hopped up on the desk, bracelets clacking against the metal. Slacker opened his eyes. "There you are. So where have you been? I was worried." A smile let her know that he was not really upset.

"First, I'd love a story. Please," she begged. Only she knew that it might be the last one. Slacker unfurled himself from the chair and rooted around for a book of records. His long fingers traveled along the dark blue ledgers stopping suddenly.

"Let's see, 1886-1890. That's where we were." He placed the huge ledger lovingly on the desk and opened it to 1887. Cedar ran her hand down the page. So many words, so much to learn, so much to do. She loved the feel of the book's heft, its scent of the past and the design the letters made across the page.

Slacker read: *"February 28, 1886; Susan VanDussel, female, Caucasian, DOB unknown but appears to be in her sixties, height 5'5", weight 165, temperature-98.7, Bp 160/95. The patient was brought in by police who reported that onlookers thought she was crazy because she was sleeping in the streets and stealing from venders.*

Upon removing her coat, what remained was a skeletal creature wrapped in layers of shabby rags. She was like a withering insect stripped of its cocoon. She screamed at us in Dutch and became combative, cutting an orderly's arm with her jagged black nails.

Sedated, we moved her to Hall six where she will undergo a plunge into freezing water and then be tied to a flat board until she submits. If she doesn't, she will be shackled and taken to Ward 11."

Slacker looked up at Cedar. "It's hard to believe, isn't it?"

"Nothing makes much sense. We went from torturing people in the 1800s for being ill to almost destroying the entire planet. We are a very strange creature. Tell me something about what it was like before, please."

For this, he opened the desk drawer and pulled out another book. This one turned out to be a photo album his mother had put together when he was young. "'A picture is worth a thousand words,' my mom used to say. Here I am at my fourth birthday party!" He pointed to a small boy with a big smile.

"This is you! And what's on fire so close to you?" Cedar was a bit horrified.

"It's my cake. Birthday cake to be exact." Cedar had never seen one. "It's really sweet like those sweetener packets we have in storage. Every year, the celebrant earns another candle on top. Here I am blowing the candles out."

He turned the page. Now, Cedar was looking at Slacker's mother and what she thought must be the father holding hands in front of a statue of a young girl sitting on what looked like a stone mushroom. Slacker stood in front of them smiling. The sky was blue, the grass a deep green, and the trees cast shadows with their leafy branches. All three smiled as if happy and carefree. "This one was taken in Central Park."

The photos went on and on, showing Cedar a glimpse of the world before it was ruined. She took it all in thinking about where she had just been. It was time to tell Slacker about their discovery.

"I have a story for you tonight, but I'm starving. Is there any food around?" Slacker went to the store room and appeared with a can of Spaghettios, her favorite. Between mouthfuls, she told him her tale of time travel. Slacker was transfixed.

As she came to the end, he said, "I don't know what to say. I am both amazed and shocked. Was it truly wilderness? You saw no roads or signs of a more modern time period?"

"None."

"Incredible. How did it happen? Was there a time portal?"

And so Cedar began again, explaining the ringing in their ears and the cool temperature and the tingling goosebumps. And then she just blurted out her decision to leave. "I plan on going back with the others to stay. They all want to. It's like starting over, a second chance, a do-over. Will you come too, please?" She held her breath.

At this moment, time stood still for them. Cedar was sure that Slacker wasn't breathing either. She let out a huge breath, grabbed both his hands and squeezed. He stared right through her.

Outside, the moon did its work riling up the river currents. Cedar turned to the huge window as the glowing moon entered the frame.

Slacker thought about:

his mother

was he too old to change?

could anyone time travel?

the pain in his knee

the rat he saw in the storage closet

Cedar's eyes

Garnal

living without Cedar

Cedar thought about:

Slacker's birthday cake
Harken
the baby
the tall man
the green grass
the delicious wind
the creature with antlers – its soft snort
the bright blue birds
Garnal

Cedar broke the silence, "We plan to meet tomorrow at noon at Garnal's fire pit ready to go. Bring what you need and a gift." Her hands slipped out of Slacker's. The moon was now dead center in the window frame. "Think about it, a new world."

He pulled her in for a big hug and promised to spend all night thinking and preparing. She took in his scent of wind and fire and books. Drifting backward toward the stairs, she entreated him again. "Please come." And then she turned and disappeared down the stairs.

Slacker sat very still. He felt afraid and realized that Cedar did not feel the same way. Youth and age, there was such a gap. He had to think. Was he afraid because he was older and understood more than Cedar and her new friends? Would his infirmities of age hold them up? Age for him had been a gradual lessening of wants. He was definitely slowing down and his joints ached. In the back of his mind, he knew what his answer would be, but he would have to think about it some more. He heard the door click at the bottom of the stairs as Cedar went on to prepare and go to bed.

A very different young girl made her way to her bedroom that night, a girl on a mission. Soon, her bed was covered with her supplies: a knife, a blanket, her pack, some cups and spoons, candles, flint, one roll of duct tape, a can of Spaghettios, a few shirts, and pants. Next, she wanted to find some useful books.

The library was moonlit but still, it was hard to see. Cedar wandered the stacks with her fingers gently running along the book spines. If you can take just one book, what should it be? She would love to take a patient ledger just for the stories but maybe she should find something more helpful.

If only she could read. I need Slacker, she thought and turned to go back and get him. Just then, as if he knew her thoughts, she heard him. He too was choosing a book. He stepped into the light at the end of the aisle, shoulders sloping, a large book in each hand.

"Take these," he said. "*Netter's Medical Illustrations, Volume 2-The Reproductive System,* and *Gray's Anatomy.* They will help you survive."

In her arms, the books were heavy, heavy with regret as she knew then that Slacker was going to stay in the present. They stared at one another, and then he turned, and she watched him exit the moonlight.

Chapter 16
Inveigle

The next morning, Sol was up first. He was psyched about the monkey idea, but how was he going to catch one or should it be two? He tied his blue bandana around his head, packed a few clothes and went to knock on Phoenix and Harken's door. "Get up you guys! Today we leave this dead world behind. Come on!" Two doors flew open, and the three faced each other, three very different people who were on a mission with no rules and no guardrails. Sol's face changed shape as his smile took possession, Harken answered him with an eye roll and Phoenix spun on her toe and flew out of the ruin into the sun with the boys in pursuit.

Their gift ideas:

Phoenix: needle and 2 spools of red and blue thread.

Harken: coffee beans-maybe he would plant them.

Sol: two monkeys.

"I am thinking we raid the old lab and set up a trap with food or maybe use Ratty?" Sol's hands flew as he explained how Ratty would be safe in a tiny cage inside the bigger one.

"Are monkeys even meat eaters?" Harken asked.

"Are you nuts? No way you can use Ratty." Right on cue, Ratty poked his head up from her pocket. His pink nose twitched as if he knew they were talking about him.

"The monkeys will be more trouble than they're worth if you ask me, unless we take just the one with the mangled arm. She's pretty tame according to Cedar." Harken leaned in and tried to touch Ratty who did an about face to the bottom of the pocket.

"Let's see what Cedar thinks." Phoenix rummaged through the crate that the Camp Head had left behind. She wondered if he even knew that they were missing from the group. She thought about fate. Was her purpose set? It felt that way. She had no lingering questions. She had to go back and this time, try to save the mother too. Returning to the mainland, to her old life seemed impossible now.

She discovered some dried packets of something that now passed for food and handed them around. It was a horrid combination of dried grains, weeds, seeds and nuts. Still, they tore into them and then filled their water bottles from the crumbling fountain.

Phoenix got busy washing the blood off her arms and clothes as the two boys headed for the Strecker Memorial Laboratory. Half of the brick building stood tall with yawning glassless windows that stretched from floor to ceiling. The other half was destroyed and just a pile of rubble. They stepped over the debris into what was once the surgery where computer chips were inserted into the monkey's brains, humans too perhaps.

One exam table still stood as if waiting for the next patient. Metal cabinets were scattered about, bent and rusted. Broken glass was everywhere. Long flat lights hung from chains, complaining in the wind.

"Hey-check this out." Harken pointed to a sign, *Authorized Staff Only.*

"Nice!" Sol's hand reached the doorknob first. He turned to Harken who was breathing over his shoulder. "Fingers crossed, I hope it's food." The handle clicked and turned easily for the first time in 38 years, and two boys from the future stepped into the past.

The small room had high windows and sunlight cut across the walls in sharp lines. The boys gazed upon rows of cabinets filled with small vials and bottles of all shapes. Small screens lined one wall. "Computers, cool." They stood in front of the screens just as the doctors and nurses had and tapped the keys, but now the screens remained black.

Harken grabbed a keyboard hanging from its cord and stuffed it in his pack. He thought he could use it to teach Cedar her letters. "Penicillin, amoxicillin, morphine, vitamin D," he read the faded labels on the vials stored in the cabinets. The contents of the vials had surely been altered by time, but he grabbed a few anyway. Filthy coffee cups congregated on a small counter next to a contraption called Nespresso.

Harken suddenly realized that beans must be here too. He flipped open the top, and there they were, crumbling, but still beans. Quickly, he transferred what was salvageable to his pocket collection.

"Hey-check this out." Sol turned the latch on what looked like a small metal safe. "Whoa, these are cool." He held up surgical tools of all shapes and sizes, still a shiny silver. They laid them out on a table and discussed which ones to take.

Harken examined a curved thick needle and jostled it in Sol's face. "This could come in handy for you, the King of Kuts. We just need to find the thread."

"King of Kuts! Hah!" Sol lunged at Harken with what was actually forceps. A short duel ensued, stirring up the years of dust. They jabbed and lunged at each other until laughter won out. It felt so good.

"Sol, look here's a ledger of some kind." Harken flipped it open and dust motes escaped into the sunlight. He read:

"3/5/2008 – 3:00 pm – 10 mg histamine for Jane Allen; CN.

3/5/2008 – 3:30 pm – 20mg morphine for Andrew Schneider stat; DB.

He fast forwarded to the end. The last entry, written on 6/11/2030 at 10:30AM for 50mg amoxicillin was unfinished.

"Was this it? Was this when it happened, when the missiles hit their targets?" Harken asked no one. They both stared at the incomplete entry, pondering that moment. Harken ran his fingers over the slanted writing and imagined the nurse looking up, still unaware that this was the last day that he or she would get up to a bright sun and go to work.

Already on another mission, Sol was rummaging through the desk drawers. "Oh yeah, here we go. Pencils. Good ole 'pencils. These would be a cool gift. And a sharpener, perfect!" He grabbed three pads of paper too and stuck them in his pack. "Maybe we should forget the monkey."

"Definitely, forget the monkey. It'll just be a pain to control. Let's get going."

As they turned to go, Sol decided to investigate the narrow tower of drawers labeled alphabetically. Drawer after drawer flew open and both boys grabbed what looked like bandages and then in the '0-Z 'drawer, they found the sutures.

"This must be what they used for sewing people up! I wonder if it is too dried out." The pillaging continued. They took it all.

Phoenix was at the fire pit when they returned. "I don't see a monkey," she said with a smile.

"It was a good idea in theory, but you know, too hard, too complicated. But we found tons of good stuff in the lab." The three discussed their gifts and how they would present them while they waited for Cedar.

Harken heard her approach on that metal concoction she called a bike, bracelets singing. He felt the fist in his chest ease up when he saw her. The little group was stronger with all present. They were about to embark on a journey into the unknown. Each knew that he or she was committed to the change, but the pact was tenuous, and it needed nurturing. The change rattled their foundation, their beliefs. Unmoored from the present, the time travelers felt good and bad at the same time. It was terrifying and exciting. And so to ease the unease, they sat in their reassuring circle with knees touching. Together, they felt better, stronger and safer.

Cedar spoke first, "Slacker isn't coming." She shook her head slightly. "I tried, but he wants to stay with Garnal. He thinks it's too much change for him to handle, but I know it's super hard for him to see us go. He's like my dad. I hate to leave him."

She sighed and her lips curled, trying to keep her tears at bay. Harken found his hand on her knee and wondered how it got there. She looked up at his blue eyes and crooked mouth and realized that he was in her future, in this new future, and that as hard as it was to believe, traveling back in time was the right thing to do.

Just then, Slacker appeared with Garnal in tow. The circle stood. Garnal stirred up the dirt with his toe. Slacker cleared his throat, "I want to say something important, but I'm not sure what that is exactly. But anyway, here goes. This is a dangerous mission, but it is also one that you must take. There is little or no future for you here, but the past can be a dangerous place too. It's full of things that you have never even heard of like the mosquito or the grizzly bear. And the Native American tribe you discovered may be accepting, or they may think that you are a threat. From what little I remember from 7th grade history class, there were hundreds of tribes which were slowly destroyed or driven west to live on barren land by the invading Europeans. My advice is to be humble, open minded, useful and follow their ways."

"What's a mosquito?" Sol asked. His voice trembled with excitement.

"It's a tiny flying insect that feeds on blood and spreads disease, a deadly predator. I remember we sprayed our skin to repel them."

"If I can, I want to come back to check on you two." Cedar was about to cry. Garnal hung his head.

"You will not return. Let's make a clean break. Promise? You can't be here and there. It will handicap the mission. You need to be all in." He scanned the motley crew representing mankind from the future. "Unless of course, you fear for your lives and then leave no man behind."

Heads nodded. Cedar turned to Garnal and reached out to him holding two gifts: a Timex watch and a catch of keys hanging from what looked like a rabbit's foot. Garnal took them and a smile shot across his face. Phoenix noticed he was missing teeth. To Slacker, Cedar gave her bike and two bracelets. He tried to smile. The group knew it was time to leave. Awkwardly, they shuffled about giving hugs and whispering goodbyes for the last time.

Then in a single file with heads spinning, they proceeded to the cave. Since Garnal had discovered it, he led the way.

Chapter 17
Second Chance

The tide was out, and the cave welcomed them with its dank smell of wet earth. Sol got to the vessel first. He was vibrating with energy, sparking almost. Cedar was right behind him. Soon, the ancient ship filled with their bounty awaited her passengers. The oars shone, the barkskin's red and black geometric figures seemed brighter as if freshly painted. Sol leapt in the stern ready to steer them into the future. Cedar snagged the other oar and sat up front. Harken and Phoenix surrendered to their spots in the middle. Slacker held on to the boat. His fingers trembled. Garnal waved. Slacker let go.

Sol dug his oar deep into the churning river and pushed off. All heads turned to the past, save Cedar. She stared straight ahead toward the future afraid that she might jump ship if she looked back. Her paddle slid into the water.

They rowed steadily in silence. The temperature dropped, the ringing in their ears commenced, and then they heard the birds. The past was noisy. A fish jumped, startling them, and once again, the shore line transformed into a tangle of green.

Trees twisted and twirled along the riverbank in majestic formations that resembled huge fortresses that might guard a magical kingdom. The dirt was a dark brown, almost black. The sky was so blue, the sun so bright, and the air so clear. Mesmerized, the four explorers drifted along the shoreline. The green parted, and a doe stepped out to the river's edge. She stood watching them with her big dark eyes. This time, the four didn't look away but drank in every detail. "I wonder if it's the same one we saw last time?" Sol turned the craft toward the shoreline.

"There!" shouted Cedar. "That's where we went ashore last time!"

"I see it!" Phoenix pointed to the spot. Sol banked his paddle to aim them toward the path. Just then, a strong gust of wind swirled around them, lifting their chins. Straight ahead, snake-like tree roots along the river edge seemed to shift, and then they saw it, right there in front of them, an entrance to a cave appeared.

Cedar and Sol held the boat steady as they all summoned their courage. Vines dangled in the opening like a beaded curtain, each strand spiraling endlessly. The leaves flickered in the sunlight: light, dark, light, dark. Just then, a very large bird parted the curtain. It paddled out with its head held high trailing seven baby birds with another large bird ending the procession. The leader had an iridescent green head and a bright yellow bill. The four newcomers stared in awe. "That's a duck, I think," said Phoenix. Meanwhile, the family of nine paddled off ignoring them completely.

Cedar shifted around so she could see her friends. "Onward?" All heads nodded. With one powerful stroke,

Sol persuaded the barkskin into the cave. As they parted the curtain, the vines bathed them in water droplets.

"Look up." Harken pointed. The ceiling of the cave was not solid. A labyrinth of roots created hundreds of openings where sunlight shot through in bold streaks like columns of gold. The cave walls shimmered. Cedar sat with the paddle in her lap taking it all in. Sol maneuvered the boat slowly through the columns of light. Harken trailed his hand in the water, and Phoenix checked on Ratty.

Again Harken said, "Look up." They were beneath a huge trunk. Sol put them in reverse so all could see. The roots came from every direction, coiling into a great knot and from the center, hung a chandelier of bones, clean and white. They sat below it, rocking gently. The bones rattled a soft tune.

Cedar thought about:

Slacker
the bird's green head
would they arrive at the same moment in time?
Garnal
her bike

Sol thought about:

the computers in the lab
how the bones had to be put there by someone else
other time travelers

Phoenix thought about:

Looking up that bird in her book
never seeing her parents again
would the baby be there?

Harken thought about:

Cedar's voice
the keyboard he wanted to give her
carving a chess piece from animal bones
food – he was starving

"Hey look, there's a place to pull up and a terrace just like the other cave!" With one stroke, Sol propelled the boat up onto the sand, and they clambered out. Once they had the boat up on the terrace, they donned their packs and bedrolls and made the short journey back through the towers of light to the opening.

The cave seemed to whisper to them in a foreign tongue. The river's soft lapping notes soothed them. Fingers trailed along wet walls of moss and stone and tree. Toes wiggled in pure cool water, eight eyes drank thirstily.

Chapter 18
Remnants

Back in the future, the sky remained gray, the ash still fell, and the island was now down to just two residents. There had been no sign of the Survival group's return, and Slacker was fine with that. He was already starting to get used to his diminished world on his tiny island.

Garnal's world remained the same, and each day ended with a hunt for treasure. Just yesterday, he'd found two silver spoons. He thought a lot about Cedar, but he wasn't sad. He wasn't sure where she went or if she would be back. Her absence left a space, but he lived in a world with no expectations living moment to moment.

Unlike Garnal, Slacker did feel sad, but he knew that he would adjust. It just took time. He felt proud to have given her the go signal with no strings attached. Long ago, he had learned that true love is not selfish. He knew that he had to set her free. To fill the void her absence created, he scoured the island for books. He would organize them all and try to find information on the 1600s so he could imagine her new life. He had already found what appeared to be a short history of Roosevelt Island. His new island routine now included a daily treasure hunt for books and visiting Garnal.

Slacker was determined to teach him survival skills. As sometime in the not too distant future, Garnal would be the island's only resident.

Chapter 19
Take Two

The time travelers burst through the leafy curtain into full sunlight. The warmth of it was delicious. All faces turned up to the impossibly blue sky. "Come on, let's go see about the baby!" Phoenix felt desperate to make sure that he was okay.

"Wait, we are going in blind, here. If things go south, let's meet at the boat and stay put until everyone returns." Harken was suddenly nervous.

"What if one of us is trapped or worse yet, killed and the others don't know it?" Sol's voice seemed squeaky. He readjusted his pack. A man of action, he would rather rush right in without much thought. He knew that too much analysis might slow the mission.

"Let's say if someone is missing, we wait at least two nights and then push on to set up on our own." Cedar didn't think she could go back, not after stepping into this verdant paradise teaming with life. Heads nodded.

"I want to go, come on, the baby!" Phoenix dug her toes into the steep incline, grabbed on to some vines and began the ascent. "I don't hear him." The scrawny ill-prepared group of now orphans scrambled up the path into the past.

Soon, Phoenix thought she spotted the small glade where the child was born. "This is it, right?" She spun around, searching for the baby.

"Yeah, I think so. I recognize those two weird trees with thick leaves. Sol knelt and ran his hands through the bed of grass. "Nothing… no blood."

The four invaders stood still. White clouds drifted overhead, birds and other wild creatures rustled in the underbrush. Nearby, a badger screamed as it pounced on a rabbit. They all jumped. The past shifted on its axis to make room for them.

Phoenix let out a big sigh and sat, the others joined her. "Okay, no baby. That means…what?"

"It means that we have returned to a different time," interrupted Cedar.

"Darn, does that change anything?" Sol stood, anxious to move on.

"Not for me." Cedar was staying.

"Let's start by offering our gifts to the local tribe if we can even find them." Harken dug in the dirt. "Look how black this is." He was thinking about his coffee beans. He wondered if beans from the future would grow in the past.

"Let's go scout around." Cedar's bracelets rattled.

"Yeah, I'm psyched to check out the past. I mean we are in a sweet spot in some ways." Sol beckoned to them.

Phoenix checked on Ratty. "It's weird, but I wanted the baby to be here."

"Maybe he's grown up now."

"Or not even born yet."

The deliberation went on as they headed down the worn path in single file.

Chapter 20
Lenape

The four explorers had already been spotted by a young Native American, Flying Bird of the Lenape Nation. A lean coyote had also noticed them but wasn't interested. Wild turkeys crisscrossed their path. Huge grasshoppers dive bombed them. The forest had taken note of their presence including Flying Bird who watched the strangers intently. He was surprised by how close he could get.

He didn't feel threatened by them. He saw no weapons, and the shiny bracelets rattling on one girl announced their procession to all. Her long brown hair was twisted in knots. The other girl had skin so pale, he thought she might be sick. He marveled at her hair which was the color of the sun. The skinny boy had skin like his and dark hair in tight curls. He couldn't just walk; he sort of hopped and skipped his way along. He made Flying Bird smile. The tall one had pure black hair like his, but it curled and curled into long worm shapes that stuck out from his head. His skin was like the girl with sun in her hair. Who were these interlopers with strange skin and hair?

Flying Bird felt his heart race. He crouched just out of sight. His education had taught him to judge the threat level of any unfamiliar beast, person or idea before engaging. He was open-minded though and raised to think that all beings are part of nature. He did not consider altering nature, he accepted it as is. Nor did he see himself as better than a bird or a caterpillar. So it followed that newcomers, once evaluated for safety, should be accepted.

He continued to shadow them with ease as they marched along in a parade. Any chance he had of finding that bear he was tracking was negated by the commotion they made. Just then, their pace slowed as they approached his tribe's fire pit. The boy who was funny danced around the dead embers while the girl with the silver arms smacked her hands together and laughed. The girl with yellow hair dug around in her pack, and the tallest boy sat down and pulled something small out of his pocket.

Flying Bird moved even closer to them. Now, the girl with sun in her hair pulled something big out of her pack, and they all sat in a tight circle around it. Their heads leaned down over it, and the girl with a ring in her nose spoke.

Her words sounded so strange to him. The funny boy spun the object to him, and he spoke. What was this thing? Now, they were all speaking. What if he just stood up and revealed himself? Flying Bird was tempted but held back. He wondered if he should head back home to warn his tribe, but he hated to leave. Perhaps he would just continue to observe and gather information. Flying Bird remained hidden.

"Let's leave our gifts here," offered Harken. He spit on his Rook and polished it on his dirty shorts.

"Yeah, here's good." Sol spun in a circle, arms out like the Lenape. One at a time, they placed their gifts within the fire circle.

Cedar: three bracelets.

Harken: a chess piece – the black knight.

Phoenix: a spool of blue thread and a needle.

Sol: a pad of yellow paper and a pencil. He drew a simple tree with four stick figures dancing around it.

"What if it rains?" said Sol worried about the paper. Cedar arranged the gifts and then took a stick and drew circle after circle around them. Sol grabbed the stick from her and drew a triangle through the circles. They all stood back and admired the offering.

Unsatisfied, Harken drew small stars at each triangle point and then Phoenix wrote the words, *we come in peace.*

"We come in peace."

"That's good I think."

"Hopefully."

"Unless it rains."

"That's the least of our worries," said Harken. "Now what?"

The spy sat nearby in the tall grass and wondered about the strangers, especially the one he had named Silver Arms. Suddenly, the group was on the move, packing up and heading back the way they had come from the river. He followed them until they disappeared into a cave in the riverbank. Flying Bird climbed out on a rocky ledge overlooking the river to wait and see what they were up to next. He studied the day's end as the sun sank behind the far hills. Colors melted into one another and became one. Everything grew softer, muted, edges dissolved. He thought about how the light slowly dies, giving darkness its turn. He was in no hurry to go anywhere. There was no schedule to worry about or appointments to keep. He sat like a monument in stony silence. He listened to the river laughing, to the trees talking and to the owl hooting. Once the moon and stars took over, he felt confident that the newcomers would stay put. Flying Bird rose, spun and flew back to his village to tell all about what he had seen.

Chapter 21
Encounter

What happens when two worlds collide? If extraterrestrials landed in your backyard, just imagine what would happen. Fear would be the initial reaction. Do we always fear what we do not understand? Why is fear our first response to the unknown?

Luckily for the Time Travelers, Flying Bird would prove to be a good emissary. But before returning to the settlement, he studied the objects that they left behind. He really wanted to touch the chess piece but restrained himself. The lines drawn in the dirt meant something, he was sure. He trailed the stick they used over them. The circle was sacred in his culture, and he wondered if it was the same for them. His heart galloped in his chest as he ran home.

His mind was full of questions. What else was in their strange packs? Why was their skin different colors? What was the big square object they all stared at? He ran faster. He was excited about the change the foursome might bring to him and to his people, the Lenape.

Flying Bird burst into his village, which consisted of twenty wigwams positioned high on a ridge overlooking the river. In the center was a fire pit with seats all around. With a loud whistle, he summoned the tribe.

His excitement was obvious as he tried to hurry everyone to their seats. The elders took their places on the logs as the younger ones squeezed in between their legs. All eyes were on Flying Bird. He took a deep breath and began. As he spoke, he maneuvered around the circle, his hands paddling in the air as he tried to describe what had happened. His words flew out, tripping over each other.

He watched the faces he loved grow wide eyed. Chief Dancing Fish rose to his feet and asked his son to draw what he had seen in the dirt. Soon all were staring at three circles, one within the other with the bisecting triangle accented with three stars.

A debate went on for hours until an agreement to conditionally accept the newcomers as visitors was reached. Sentinels were sent out to keep watch, and a pipe went around the circle. Few slept that night in anticipation of what tomorrow would bring.

Back in the cave, the four from the future huddled together, ate what they had and tried to sleep. The barkskin sat waiting patiently for its next trip through time.

Back in the future, Slacker helped Garnal lock up for the night and then headed home. He thought about trying to move Garnal to the tower or perhaps he would set up a place where he could sleep at the station. Then his thoughts turned to Cedar. He missed her so much, it felt like he was sick. Tonight, he would read from the hospital records but to no one. He so wished that he would hear from the four explorers, but he knew he had to let that go.

Back on the mainland, chaos prevailed. It wasn't safe, no one was sure who to trust. The small Survival Challenge group was preparing to return to the island after dealing with a student's broken wrist. The Camp Director had made the decision to leave Phoenix, Sol and Harken behind as it was an emergency, but he needed to get back to them quickly. Little did he know that he would never see them again. His thoughts were full of what ifs.

We all have 'what ifs 'that tease us.

What if we knew what the future held for us?

What if the Lenape knew that European invaders would destroy their paradise?

What if the Head of Camp knew that he had lost the three left behind forever?

What if the Time Travelers knew that they would play a role in history?

The next morning, the four Travelers from 2064 woke to a rhythm drummed by Lenape men from the 1600s. Their weathered hands beat on the stretched deer hide telling a story about how the earth does not belong to man. Instead, man belongs to the earth, and the newcomers belong to the earth too so it follows that they must belong with them.

The village stirred early and quickly completed its morning rituals of bathing in the river and praying to the sun as it rose so they could go and see what the strangers had left behind. Dancing Fish pressed them to hurry. He paced around the wigwams with Flying Bird at his side.

Nearby, Sol tried to rally the group to action. "I bet they've found the gifts!" He shouted. "Come on, let's go see!" He rolled off the ledge and landed like a cat.

"Maybe," Phoenix answered. She sat cross legged on the stony ledge and opened her big book, positioning it just beneath a shaft of sunlight. The white pages turned to stop at: *Native American,* again.

As she read silently, the others joined her, knees touching. "Darn, there's nothing here about drumming."

Sol snapped his fingers. "Come on, this is it. Let's go see if they took the gifts."

Harken placed his hand on the page, and three more followed his lead, a small stack of innocence. "This is it for us, our shot at a future exists in the past. That feels weird just to say it. Our future is in the past. Nuts."

The hands remained. "To the past!"

"To the future!"

"To future's past or past futures."

"Our future lies in the past. That should be our motto!" Cedar grinned.

The hands rose and fell as all chanted, "Our future lies in the past."

The book slammed shut and Sol stood. "Remember, we come back here and wait for the others if something happens." He handed out some dried grasshoppers to eat.

"No matter what. We wait for each other." Cedar reached for her share.

The small procession made its way through the golden shafts of sunlight in silence. The walls seemed to vibrate. The air tasted green, and the water felt electric. Four brains, four hearts, and one mission burst into the sunlight.

Cedar thought about:

Harken's hand
Slacker
Garnal
her bike
the baby

Sol thought about:

learning to hunt
meat
the sound of the river
the baby – were they in time?

Phoenix thought about:

the tall man's voice
the red birds that crisscrossed her path
the dead mother's face
the baby's perfect fingers

Harken thought about:

Cedar's hand
their timeline – was the baby born?
had they arrived years before or after?
his father waving goodbye
food

Sol led out again and Harken brought up the rear of the line which curled its way through the massive trees toward the clearing. Suddenly, the leader paused, and his hand went up signaling them to stop. "Listen."

The forest serenaded them with a symphony of bird calls and mysterious sounds of creatures scavenging in the underbrush. To the Time Travelers, it was a land of wonder never before experienced. A flock of goldfinches swooped down like a thousand small suns lighting their way. To their right, a herd of white tail deer stood motionless. Their heads were up, ears twitching like antennae, brown eyes wide, watching. A white tail swished, and they flew into a tangle of angular limbs as they leapt to safer ground.

Far above the canopy, a flock of geese flew in their V formation honking out their discordant refrains. The newcomers stared up at the sky. A huge groundhog waddled across their path, and Cedar's hand went to her knife. She wanted to eat. Her mouth watered. But she knew this was not the moment. Just then, Sol lowered his hand, and they proceeded toward what they hoped would be their future.

The drumming stopped. "I smell fire," whispered Phoenix.

"Me too."

"Here we go."

They huddled in the tall grass at the edge of the clearing. A thin line of smoke rose from the fire pit. The tribe had come. They had taken the gifts, yet the clearing was empty. A short discussion decided that they would stay together and all go to investigate the circle.

Harken's hand shot out and three joined his. They whispered, "Our future lies in the past."

As they approached the fire, it became clear that it wasn't just a fire but food sizzled above it in a clay pot. They stood on the edge of the circle and took it in: the smell, their missing gifts and a new circle drawn three times around the pit. Small bowls and roughly carved spoons sat ready for them. Harken pointed to four figures drawn in the dirt. They were holding hands. "Wait, how do they know there are four of us?"

"I bet they've been watching us," said Sol. He searched the edges of the clearing but saw nothing.

"That's weird but of course, they should be watching us." Cedar studied the four figures drawn in the dirt. "That's me. See, they put lines around my arms for the bracelets."

"Cool. I bet that's me with the crazy hair." Harken smiled.

"I'm starving, let's eat. If it's poisoned, it's poisoned," announced Sol.

"I'm with you," answered Phoenix.

Hunger took over, and their packs dropped. Skinny arms and filthy hands hovered over the pot, bowls filled up and the four starving creatures slurped up the stew filled with meat and fish. They sat, knees touching as always and ate in silence except for the occasional groan of pleasure.

The tribe watched them from a safe distance. Flying Bird held his breath. His father gave the signal, and they very slowly emerged from the trees in the form of a circle. The newcomers, engrossed in their first meal in ages, didn't look up or hear them.

The tribe stopped at about twenty feet away from its nucleus and waited. Cedar, the hunter, felt them first and put her bowl down. Harken looked at her and then beyond. Sol and Phoenix followed suit.

No one spoke. No one moved. Except for Ratty, he poked his pink nose out from Phoenix's pocket and sniffed the crisp air.

Flying Bird's head flew back, and he barked out a laugh. At that, the outer circle came alive. Everyone was talking and pointing at them. The inner circle put down their bowls and stood. The one who struggled to speak in the past, spoke first. *What was going on with him,* wondered Harken. His mouth was moving, words were tumbling out. Suddenly, he was all talk, and he liked it. "Thank you so much for this meal." He held up his bowl. Sol pantomimed eating and rubbed his belly as Ratty nibbled his way through some leftovers. All four held up their bowls, nodded their heads and said thank you. Cedar's bracelets sparkled in the sun. Dancing Fish thought she looked like a butterfly.

Without a script, Harken launched into their story. He seemed to have developed a magical power. This time, the girls helped Sol pantomime the words. Harken began the story many years ago when the missiles were launched and the grids went down and the climate sputtered to a slow crawl toward disaster.

They acted out a big explosion, and Sol threw himself to the ground and rolled about. Their captive audience laughed. It was not what he was going for, but still, it was a positive reaction.

As they pretended to paddle from the future to the past, the tribe erupted into a discussion as this was something that they recognized. Dancing Fish had no idea really what the pantomime meant, but his instinct told him that these were good creatures, dirty and scrawny but good. Their gifts were mysterious, and he wanted to know more about them. As chief of a Lenape tribe, he valued generosity rather than wealth. He twirled the black chess piece in his hand as he watched the impromptu show.

When they pantomimed arriving on the island, Flying Bird caught on. Suddenly, he recognized the part of the story he had witnessed and joined in. He crouched down and mimicked sneaking through the tall grass to spy on them, which inspired the circle to once again erupt into laughter. Everyone was having fun now.

Harken ended the story with a reenactment of them drawing the circles and placing the gifts. Then they stood shoulder to shoulder, held hands and did a quick bow. Flying Bird stood and returned to stand next to his father.

Dancing Fish stepped forward and spoke. His deep voice was like a smooth wave gently washing over them. His hands gestured and seemed to envelop them with hope. Just then, the circle disintegrated and everyone seemed to be heading off into the woods.

Dancing Fish raised his right hand and indicated that they should follow. The Time Travelers grabbed their packs and went in pursuit of their new life. At least, they were invited to visit.

Later that day as the sun set, the four newcomers gathered around the small fire in their new digs, a dome shaped structure made of saplings and elm tree bark. The smoke twirled up through the hole in the top. Their day had been spent meeting everyone. Young and old, there seemed to be about thirty or so people in this village. "I feel so lucky, it's almost like a miracle. Isn't it?" Cedar started the conversation.

"Hopefully, they seem so kind," said Phoenix. "They even like Ratty."

"Yeah, and peaceful," Sol shook his head.

"Did you notice the pregnant woman with the scar on her face?" said Phoenix.

"That's got to be her, what do you think?" Sol searched the six eyes that watched him.

Phoenix tossed her bedding on the floor as exhaustion was upon her. "I've got to sleep, there's too much to think about."

Cedar stretched out on her bed roll. "It's her."

"It's weird knowing her future. I don't like it." Phoenix closed her eyes.

"Me either, but that's why we are here, right?" Cedar was determined to change history.

"It's nuts, all of it." Sol rolled around on this blanket trying to find comfort.

Harken was the last man sitting. "We all die. We all know that it will happen but knowing when it will happen is torture." No one seemed to be listening, so he joined the others and slid under his blanket, mind racing. "How did we evolve from these gentle people into the greedy creatures who ruined the planet? When did we decide that we own the land we live on? I have so many questions," he whispered to no one.

Then, a whisper came from Cedar, "Did you see the size of that rodent? And what about the yellow birds?" Cedar felt like she had landed in a dream.

"Amazing, all of it." Harken thought about how Cedar's bracelets warbled a tune as she settled in to sleep.

"I don't want to know when I will die. Do you?"

"No way." Harken rolled over to face Cedar.

"Do you think we made the right decision?"

"Yes."

"Good, me too."

Exhaustion took over, and the four slept in their birch bark home nestled on a ridge overlooking the East River, some four hundred years before they were born.

Chapter 22
Naked

Early the next morning, their door flap flew open, and a girl about their age motioned for them to follow her. Her black hair was pulled back into a thick braid intertwined with white and gray feathers. She led them to the river. It was a misty morning, and the sun had just begun to light the east. She slipped out of her leather dress, took three steps into the water and vanished beneath the surface.

The four stood transfixed by the disappearing act. They waited. Sunlight penetrated the mist and tinted the morning a greenish gold. Time dragged on. It seemed like forever, but then she broke the surface like a glistening fish, gasping for air. Flinging her head back, the braid sent droplets flying through the green mist like shooting stars. The four stared. It was too beautiful – the river, the light, the mist, the girl. As she picked her way to the shore, the newcomers got busy taking off their clothes.

Harken kept his eyes down. Cedar let her flimsy shorts and shirt drop and then shot into the river. Sol shook his head and followed suit revealing his myriad of battle scars. Phoenix raced into the river in her clothes and then took them off.

"Good idea Phoenix." Cedar disappeared underwater.

"This will be great. Naked is cool. Right? We'll get used to it." Sol splashed Harken who then dove under water and attacked his legs. A short wrestling match set everyone laughing.

Early Bird, their young guide, gathered up their filthy clothes and replaced them with a clean Lenape wardrobe. She wondered about their skin colors. Each one was so different from the other. The funny boy had skin darker than hers and black hair that curled tightly to his head. The girl with a ring in her nose had very pale skin and hair like the sun. Silver arms had skin like her, but her hair was brown, and her eyes were a greenish brown. The boy who told the story had pale skin with a reddish tint and long black hair that curled into bouncing snakes. She couldn't wait to find out more about them.

Meanwhile, the Time Travelers felt trapped in the water by their nakedness. Harken stared at the four piles of clothing on shore. It suddenly seemed like a long way to go. Time seemed to stand still as they emerged from the river, naked before all. With eyes averted, they struggled to put on their new garb. But soon – loin cloth and all – the four were dressed and smiling at each other.

Sol thought they looked fantastic. "I love these!"

"The leather is so soft!" Phoenix found a pocket for Ratty, and he snuggled into his new home.

The sun continued its ascent and lit the underbelly of the clouds orange and pink. The Lenape girl spoke telling them to face east and pray as the sun rose. She turned and raised her face to the sun.

"Just do what she does. Look, others are doing the same." Sol encouraged them. And so they stood facing east on the first morning of their new future.

Harken thought about:

Cedar's wet hair stuck to her back
the barkskin waiting for them in the cave
carving a new chess piece
the coffee beans

Phoenix thought about:

braiding her hair like the Lenape
the pregnant woman
her book – safe in the pack

Sol thought about:

breakfast
his new duds – loved them
breakfast again

Cedar thought about:

where to store her knife
the water droplets tickling her back
the birds soaring over the river
learning to use a bow & arrow

Chapter 23
Lessons

Soon, they were trying their best to fit in as everyone returned to the village center where bowls of dried meat and berries awaited them. All eyes were on the newcomers as they ate. It became apparent that they were first on the day's agenda. The chief wanted to discuss their offerings and had them lined up in front of him. He welcomed them again and thanked them for the gifts. Today, his long black hair was twisted into two braids wrapped in leather laces with blue feathers entwined. His leather tunic was decorated with red, white and black beads in geometric shapes. Around his neck hung a turtle shell with white beads embedded around the perimeter. To the Time Travelers, he looked like a King.

Dancing Fish held up the black knight chess piece and spoke again. Harken unzipped his backpack. The circle leaned in to see. It occurred to Harken that they had never seen a zipper. He zipped it back and forth showing them the purpose and method. He held it up for them to touch. Early Bird felt bold and tried pulling it back and forth. She smiled at Harken. Cedar stepped in between them as he arranged the chess game for all to see. Harken enjoyed the slow reveal of the two armies. One by one, the chess pieces took their positions on their assigned squares. The makeshift board was made of a heavy white cloth painted with crude black squares.

As Harken mimed how one played chess, he found himself thinking about how odd this scene was. He wondered how he, a being from the future, was teaching the Lenape, a people from the past, a game that began in 600 AD, long before either of them existed. He was thinking too much. Meanwhile, old and young tried moving the pieces about with much joy and laughter.

Phoenix was next. She held up her sewing needle for all to see. Then she threaded it and held it between her teeth. Next, she grabbed a shirt from her pack and ripped it. Now, she had their rapt attention. It seemed that they were all turning into performers. Quickly, her needle dove in and out of the cotton until the shirt was once again whole. She held up her work and tugged at the new seam. The old white t-shirt went around the circle.

There was much Lenape discussion as they felt the fabric and held it up to the light. Phoenix pulled Sol to her and mimed sewing up a scar on his arm. This brought on more debate. Satisfied, she sat down and now, it was Cedar's turn.

Cedar wasn't sure how to explain her weird collection of found jewelry and homemade bracelets made from metal refuse. There was no metal here yet. So, she took them off and passed them around for all to try.

Sol was next. He was thinking about how to demonstrate the written word. He began by drawing a rough sketch of Flying Bird on the yellow paper. Beneath it he wrote: *For my new friend*. He ripped the page from the pad with great fanfare, and it flew around the circle. Everyone was talking and pointing and laughing. Flying Bird posed like the sketch and grinned. The message though was still a mystery to them as the Lenape people did not have a written language.

The Time Travelers struggled to find a way to explain how the sounds you make can be translated to figures drawn on a page. Just then, Phoenix found herself pulling the huge book out of her pack. There was a collective gasp from the circle as they all moved closer to see. The cover was a deep red, tarnished and creased. Its golden title, faded by time, decorated the front. Phoenix wondered what they thought it was. She sat cross legged to begin their ritual. Sol, Harken and Cedar joined her, and they sat knee to knee as always with the book in the middle. Just then, Dancing Fish leaned over and touched Phoenix's shoulder. She looked up into his kind brown eyes. He indicated that he too would like to be in the circle. And so he and a few others inserted themselves. Everyone else formed a larger circle around them and leaned in to see and hear.

Phoenix opened the book and turned the pages until she came to Native American. She read, "*Native Americans also known as the American Indian are the indigenous people who inhabited the Americas before the Europeans arrived. There are 574 recognized tribes within the US. Their ancestors arrived in what is now the United States at least 15.000 years ago from Asia via Beringa.*" Her finger trailed along the lines pausing at the sketch of a Native American woman and man. The couple stood solemnly side by side.

Flying Bird turned the book to him as he had seen them do and touched the picture, and the others did the same. Phoenix pulled the book around to her again and turned to page 338 to the word – *fox*. She was sure there was a picture. She held up the book and pointed to the small drawing and all nodded their heads in recognition. Then she read, "*The fox is a small to medium sized omnivorous mammal belonging to the family Canidai. Foxes have a flattened skull, upright ears, a pointed, slightly upturned snout, and a bushy tail or brush.*"

Meanwhile, Sol had an idea and leapt up to draw a tree in the dirt. "Tree," he said. Many repeated him.

The woman with gray braids said the Lenape word for tree, and the Time Travelers repeated it. Sol wrote the letters T-R-E-E and sounded them out one by one. The tribe was laughing now as he danced about.

Cedar meanwhile was just now noticing that there were children of all ages skipping about. They kept running up and touching her silver arms. They encircled Phoenix too. One snatched Ratty and held him in her hand.

It was turning into a party and everyone relaxed. The lesson was over. *To be continued,* thought Harken. He couldn't wait for the next challenge.

Chapter 24
Katami

The party broke up and everyone returned to his or her work for the day. Phoenix kept her eye on the pregnant woman and followed her to what evolved into a hunt for berries and herbs. They meandered a narrow path, stopping here and there to uncover and pick a variety of plants. Phoenix, who came from a world with very few plants, had no idea what they were. Suddenly, the young woman leaned over with her hands on her knees and took a deep breath. Phoenix touched her shoulder, and the Native woman turned to face her. They were about the same height. Blue eyes stared into brown.

With gestures and repetition, they learned each other's names. Katami took Phoenix's hand and placed it on her stomach. The life within moved and Phoenix jumped. Two heads flew back and both laughed. Phoenix gently tried again. It felt like a miracle, tiny feet and fists poking out at the world, "I'm here!"

Remember me, we've met once before. Phoenix pressed lightly on what she imagined was his foot. Tears appeared as her thoughts returned to the bloody scene of his future birth. She thought about his tiny body curled up against her chest, his tiny perfect fingers, and his tiny perfect toes.

As they sat and shared a few berries, Phoenix studied her new companion. Her deep brown eyes seemed lit with tiny stars. Her softly planed face was divided equally by a regal nose. Her skin was silky smooth and glistened a bit. The scar on her forehead was an old one and ran from the edge of her scalp on the upper left side to her right brow. Her plump lips grabbed at the berries like two hungry worms. It was so hard for Phoenix to believe that Katami would die in childbirth. Then she thought, *what if this was not the birth that they came upon but an earlier child, a birth that she will survive. This was getting way too complicated.*

Meanwhile, Katami wasn't worried about anything. The Lenape didn't try to control nature. If something happened, it happened. She lived in the moment, pulling up mushrooms, smelling the soft black earth as it fell away from the roots, noticing the stone beneath her soft moccasin, and then the sharp cry of a fox joined by the keen of a hawk high overhead.

She existed among these things, she was part of the woods, part of the birds and part of the mushrooms. Her world was less complicated than Phoenix's. She did not think about the future or worry about the past. She did not wonder about what she should do next or if what she did was important. All things were equal to her: work, play, sun, fish, water, tree, fox, snow, Katami.

Phoenix thought about:

the baby inside Katami
their ship hidden in the cave
would they stay
would they go
could she save Katami's life

Katami thought about:

her new friend's pale skin
the weight of her satchel
her baby
red berries
sharing berries with birds
the gray hare watching them

Back at the village, Harken and Sol had been recruited to learn the art of flint knapping, and Cedar had managed to head out with a hunting party. Harken watched Cedar until she disappeared into the foliage. He wished that he was with her.

The small hunting party of five set out in single file on a well-worn path. To the tribe, Cedar seemed to be the leader of her small party. She wore silver on her arms and legs, and the tallest boy followed her everywhere. She had been invited to join them to honor her rank even though females did not usually hunt.

To Cedar, her new tribe was magnificent. They moved silently with grace and economy. Predators in a complicated landscape: thinking, adjusting, calculating. In comparison, she felt like a huge lumbering creature. Quickly, she realized that her bracelets were too loud; she slid them off and hung them on a tree branch. Just then, a raised hand halted the line. The hand signaled left and right, and the line divided.

Cedar followed Flying Bird. His long black hair hung to his waist. He carried a bow as tall as she was in his left hand. His leather quiver held six arrows fletched with yellow and white feathers. He stopped and pointed, her eyes traveled down his lean arm and there in a small clearing, she saw the target innocently pecking at the dirt.

It was a huge bird at least half her height and very round. It had long legs, a small head, and a red neck. As she stared at this strange creature, another waddled into sight and another. Maybe it wasn't a bird. Cedar got her knife out.

She heard Flying Bird slide an arrow into place. He pulled back on the bow string, took aim and let go. There was a whistling sound and then a shriek followed by a great commotion as the creatures exploded into an awkward flight.

Birds, she thought. The small clearing was a dark mass of beating wings. Cedar heard the zing of other arrows on their way, and then the thud as one found its target. The huge bird seemed to stall in mid-flight and then it plummeted to the ground like a feathery bomb.

A sharp whistle rang out, and the hunting party emerged from the underbrush to evaluate and gather their bounty. Two arrows had struck one bird which seemed to cause much discussion, and then the four men measured the distance between the arrows. If Cedar had understood Lenape customs, she would have known that a judgment is called for when more than one arrow takes down an animal. The owner of the arrow closest to its heart gets the choicest parts for his family. She would have also known that each hunter had his arrows fletched with specific colors just for this purpose. Once the victor was determined, two men headed back to the village with the birds in tow leaving Cedar, Flying Bird and a hunter named Turtle to continue.

Turtle was older than Flying Bird but still a young man. His hair was pulled straight back into a single braided ponytail, thick and shiny like a serpent. He had painted a red line down the middle of his face. He handed her a spear and indicated how to throw it. Cedar was thrilled. This was a beautiful instrument compared to what she had engineered at home. Just thinking about home threw her off balance. *This is home now*, she thought. *I am hunting in a forest.* All of it was almost too much, too good.

The wind rustled in the canopy. Small birds darted along the path almost like companions or guides. She was starting to feel more connected to the hunt, to the path, to the trees, and to the spear which balanced nicely in her right hand. And so the party of three proceeded, perhaps the first Lenape hunting party to ever include a girl from the future. Turtle thought she looked too skinny to be strong, but she would prove to be just the opposite.

Cedar spotted the deer first. It was a young male, his rack just beginning to sprout. She reached out and touched Turtle's back. He froze mid step and looked back, she pointed.

Cedar raised the spear, and Turtle nodded his head indicating that she should take a shot. Flying Bird nocked his arrow. Cedar calculated the distance to the deer's heart, her strength, the weight of the spear, and the arc of its flight. The target raised his head in alarm. His pointed ears twitched. *Did it hear them? No time to think, just act,* thought Cedar. Her mind cleared. She reared back, took two steps and launched the spear, imagining the projectile of its flight as she let go at just the right point.

Flying Bird's arrow hit the target first, right in the chest, followed immediately by her spear which penetrated just behind the front leg. There was a strangled cry as the beast went to his knees and then collapsed.

Cedar wanted to shout, but she controlled her joy and followed their lead as they approached the kill. The arrow was definitely aimed directly at the heart so there was no measuring. Turtle and Flying Bird thanked the deer for giving up its life for them as was Lenape custom while Cedar looked on.

Soon, they were threading their way home with the kill dangling from her spear. Cedar thought about her bracelets and hoped that she could remember where she put them. The day flew by, filled with a variety of jobs including skinning, gutting and preparing their bounty to eat. Cedar did her part and the hunters were impressed.

Later, around a fire, stories were told. The four newcomers let the soothing Lenape words flow over them. Much of the storytelling was about them and the mysteries they brought with them. Then, Dancing Fish beckoned for Harken to stand. The Chief wanted to hear another one of his stories. Harken seemed different to him now with his shirt off and thick black curls pulled back into a knot. He looked like *he* might be the chief.

Harken was surprised to find himself standing and about to speak to an entire tribe. He stared around the circle. All eyes were on him. He took a deep breath, stole a glance at Cedar and began the story that he would build upon and tell many times.

He spoke of his parents, what little he remembered about them, his kind father and ambitious mother. He described what was left of the huge city that would be built right here on their island and how the war had transformed the dying planet into a jungle of polluted remains all because mankind became too greedy and forgot about what was important.

He explained how people of the future treasured objects. Mankind liked to own things, and he thought he was superior to all animals and to all of nature. The story included the Survival Camp, meeting Cedar, their discovery in the cave and then the trip that ended right here at this circle where he stood telling a story to a people from long ago who didn't understand his words.

He spoke of both trips in the canoe but left out the part about stumbling upon Katami and the baby. And as would become their custom, his tiny troupe of three acted out the story.

The Lenape paid close attention, and when Harken concluded and sat down, drummers tapped out a soft rhythm almost like a whisper. If the four interlopers had understood, they would have known that this was telling a story of the turtle, their tribe's main symbol. The Lenape admired the turtle, especially its slow pace which allows for contemplation and reason. But do not underestimate the turtle as it is a mighty fortress when it needs to be, impenetrable if attacked.

Later that night when the four circled up in their wigwam, they discussed what they had learned that day. The main focus was on Katami. How could they determine if this was the birth that they stumbled upon? It became clear that this pregnancy could be an earlier one that was successful. Phoenix shook her head. "I guess it would help if we find out if she has any other children."

Just then, Cedar remembered the books Slacker had given her and dragged them out. Now, four heads leaned over *Netter's Medical Illustrations Volume 2, a book* for physicians about the reproductive system.

"Yikes, this is amazing but super weird too," mumbled Sol. He wanted to turn the page, but the next one was just as graphic.

Cedar looked up at him and said, "I wonder if Slacker knew that we would eventually need this information for us. I mean if we survive to have kids."

Curious fingers turned the pages which revealed every detail of the human body inside and out. Male and female genitalia seemed to be on every one. They were both hungry for what the pictures would teach them and shocked by how little they understood. Chuckles, winces, jabs and groans went around the circle as the facts were laid bare, literally.

"Check out this picture," Harken pointed to one showing a baby's head crowning. Everyone stared.

"Whoa, that looks like one of those things we found in the lab," Sol jumped up and grabbed his pack. He laid out the shiny tools that they had taken. This is it! He held up the forceps. He twirled the silver instrument and then lunged at their knees with it.

The wigwam filled with nervous and then hysterical laughter. They rolled around and laughed until they cried.

Harken thought about:

playing chess with Flying Bird
the flint he attempted to make
blood tripping from the deer as they slit it open
Cedar's beaming smile
blood streaked across her face

Sol thought about:

the baby curled up inside Katami
him curled up inside his mother
why didn't the baby need to breathe
learning to drum

Phoenix thought about:

Katami
her brown eyes full of stars
her soft voice
the force of the baby's foot pushing against her hand

Cedar thought about:

the spear
the clearing full of feathers

making a bow
her bracelets, she had to find them

The night ended with all hands in and their motto, "Our future lies in the past."

Chapter 25
Quotidian

With each day came new miracles for the Time Travelers: blue butterflies fluttering in a field of orange flowers, thick black snakes winding up trees, lush red berries adorning mossy paths, silky white spider webs festooning every branch. Slowly, their new world revealed itself to them.

The newcomers jumped in to tribal life. Everyone had daily chores, and all work was divided up equally. Play was part of everyday too. Soon family units started to become apparent. They found out that Katami was married to Gray Wolf, and that this was her first child. All good news for the Time Travelers who were about to add something to the mix of daily activities.

It all started with a small circle and *Netter's* illustrated medical book. Phoenix encouraged Katami to be her model, and then she opened to the page showing the baby curled up inside the womb.

The Lenape audience had no idea what they were seeing. It made no sense. They crawled closer and touched the detailed anatomical cross section of a pregnant uterus. Phoenix touched Katami's belly and then pointed to the picture.

Sol read the captions and labels. The circle burst into a conversation between themselves and then indicated that they would like to see more. Phoenix turned to the page illustrating the crowning head as the baby is about to be born. All stared in silence.

Then she turned to a page with a cross section of the female body minus the baby. Fingers ran up and down the shiny page tracing the arteries and veins and muscles and bones. Phoenix stood and Sol pointed to parts of her body and then at its corresponding part in the illustration. "The heart is here, and the lungs here." The lesson went on, and the students were hooked. They wanted to see every page. And so began a new ritual for the tribe.

Another circle formed around Harken and Cedar and the age-old game of chess. Cedar had never played, but she caught on quickly. The black and white figures moved about their little stage, each piece following its specific route determined by people 1000 years before. As Harken took Cedar's pieces one by one, the crowd cheered and rooted for both. They pointed and wondered and laughed. Finally, the White King fell, Harken had won. He shook Cedar's hand as was customary after a game. The touch shot through him; he didn't want to let go.

Harken motioned for someone else to play. The audience looked skeptical, and then Gray Wolf sat down to give it a try. He was lean without being skinny. His thick mane was pulled up high and secured in a leather band and then braided. He stared into Harken's eyes searching for signs of what to do, what to expect.

Harken went over the goal of the game and how each figure moved. Gray Wolf's knitted brow revealed his intense concentration. This game went slowly as Gray Wolf tried to find a path to Harken's King. Harken was a patient teacher. He let Gray Wolf win a few pieces, and when he did, his face lit up with a wide smile. He'd let out a whoop that made Harken jump. Everyone laughed and chattered away, but in the end, Harken closed in and took his King.

White Otter sat down next and others followed. A small boy named Two Wolf lined up the pieces perfectly as they fell. Another little girl named Blue Sky played with the pieces like dolls.

An older man named Wise Crow joined the circle with a carving knife and some tree limbs. It was already clear to him which two pieces were missing. He spoke to Harken and began to carve. Perhaps they would make many new chess sets, and he would teach them all to play. As always, Harken's mind was swirling with thoughts and questions. Would this tribe evolve differently because of them? Would they learn to speak English before the English arrived? Why should he encourage them to learn what he knew? Would his good fortune end up hurting the tribe? Did Cedar like him? He couldn't stop thinking about her.

Chapter 26
Frog Moon

At the next full moon, Frog Moon, another hunting party formed and this time, all of the Time Travelers were invited. The tribe had given up on determining who was the chief of their small group. The Lenape spent no time wondering about where these interlopers came from or why they came. They accepted whatever the day presented with an open and compassionate mind.

The night before the hunt, the tribe gathered for a ceremony around the campfire. Drums beat out a rhythm of anticipation, and the four newcomers sat trance-like watching. Above them, the black sky studded with an endless number of stars, shimmered. They seemed to blink on and off. Shooting stars slashed the dark canvas leaving trails of light.

The moon was so big that it seemed as if they could reach up and touch its glowing face. There were no satellites in this sky, no space stations, no pollution obscuring their view.

Beneath them, the earth opened up to spring's encouragement. Sprouts wriggled up through the warm dirt to find the light and roots wriggled down to find water and nutrients. The earth seemed to vibrate with heartbeats, heartbeats of the crow, elk, rabbit and man. Listen carefully, said the drums. Listen for the sound of the heart and then let loose the arrow. It will find its way to the mark. The tribe rose to dance. The newcomers stood just outside the circle of dancers. Cedar nudged Phoenix indicating that they should join in, but Phoenix felt unsure and nudged her back. *You go first,* she thought.

Around them flowed their new family, twirling and chanting to the flames that leapt and curled and snapped between them. Their faces hung limp; their eyes were closed. Chants grew louder and then drifted to soft whispers. Arms reached out, fingertips met. Dancing Fish waved to the newcomers, beckoning them to join.

Sol spun into the circle first, his arms wide. He closed his eyes and let the rhythm take him. The drums held him captive. He felt like he could dance forever. Just then a splash of silver shattered around the circle as Cedar joined in. Harken followed, and then Phoenix drifted into the dance. She was like a tiny yellow comet orbiting the fire.

As the Lenape danced, they imagined the hunt and sent good energy into the forest. They thanked the animals for aiding in their survival. Meanwhile, the newcomers felt the joy of belonging tighten around them. They had never belonged anywhere before. And now, they seemed to be part of something much bigger than themselves, something as big as nature. The four let go of all of their worries and doubts and just danced.

Finally, they were in the moment. The circle of celebrants vibrated as one beast, spinning and chanting. Hands searched, hair entwined, sweat flew. Around them, the nocturnals rose to power. Nearby, a badger pounced upon a mole venturing out of his burrow while a Great Horned Owl looked on. Bats crisscrossed just above them, talons tore into flesh, a fox slashed throats, rabbits screamed, a wolf howled. Hearts beat.

Chapter 27
The Accident

Early the next morning, a hunting party of seven set out. Phoenix did not go. Hunting was not her thing, and she had plenty to do with keeping track of Katami and trying to educate the Lenape people and herself about human anatomy and childbirth. Her task was huge. Phoenix thought about preventing Katami's death constantly.

The Lenape people left the decision of who would live and who would die to nature. The idea of influencing one's fate did not occur to them. They saw themselves as part of nature, not smarter than or on a higher level than it. They took just what was needed to survive and did it in a way that caused no harm. They understood what modern man would forget as he fell victim to ownership and the accumulation of so-called wealth.

Sol adjusted his quiver and slid his new knife into his belt. Was he ready, could he kill to eat? He thought so. It seemed acceptable to him now, now that he needed to hunt to eat.

Harken fletched his last arrow and pulled his hair back into a messy bun so he could see. He was scared and excited at the same time. He tested the tension of his bow and practiced nocking an arrow.

Cedar pulled her leather belt tighter and removed her silver armor leaving just one bracelet on each wrist; she was getting leaner. She visualized the hunt, and imagined herself tracking prey in the forest. She was ready.

Three Stars, a tall man with three small scars on his right cheek, dipped his fingers into a small clay pot and painted red lines down each forehead and nose. Now, it was time to go.

Seven brains and seven hearts entered the forest each on a private journey and yet working together toward a common goal. As they slipped beneath the green canopy, the world grew hushed as if all who resided there were watching them.

The Lenape hunters seemed to almost disappear into the leafy landscape. Cedar wasn't far off the mark as she had been hunting since she was able. She now moved more like a creature of the path, of the tree, of the river. Sol and Harken were certainly attempting to be stealthy, but they still created a lot of noise.

Three Star's hand went up, he knelt and touched the ground. There was some whispered debate, and then they pushed on deeper and deeper into the beating heart of the forest. Cedar felt like she was being swallowed up by a green sea. Soft pine needles and huge veined leaves brushed against her face. It smelled sharp and clean. Was it minty? She became aware of her breath: in for four counts and out for eight.

Harken stayed right behind and in step with her. He pretended that they were one creature. Sol was just behind the leader. As he walked, he felt his senses open up to his new surroundings.

Again, the procession halted to examine scat and search for tracks. Three Stars handed the scat back to Sol. Sol rolled it around in his hand and took a good sniff. Not bad really, kind of like dead leaves. The scat made its way back for the newcomers to examine. Then the snaking line moved on until Sol's hand went up. He heard movement. Everyone froze. The sound got louder and seemed to come from every direction.

Suddenly, the forest vibrated with thrashing hooves and grunts. The Lenape quickly positioned themselves and drew their bows. Harken spun in a circle; he couldn't see what was making the noise. Sol followed Flying Bird and drew.

Cedar saw a flash of black. She recognized it as a wild pig from a book Slacker had read to her. Their shrieks and squeals came from every direction; these were savage fighters who would do anything to survive.

Birds and other small animals exited the scene. Cedar's cerebellum lit up. Synapses fired as she pulled up bits of the story about a King hunting pigs. There was a drawing she remembered with the young King on one knee holding his spear with one end dug into the earth. She took action.

Cedar found an open spot and knelt, she shoved the end of her spear into the ground and held it at a 45-degree angle. She shouted to Harken to get behind her, right behind her. She pushed her back into his knees, and he instinctively gripped her sides with his legs. Now she was wedged between his legs, and he drew his bow above her. She held the spear ready. Harken wasn't sure what she was up to, but there was no time for discussion.

Just then, a pig broke through the edge of the clearing, it already had an arrow dangling from its side. Mad with pain, it charged Cedar and Harken in a rage. Harken's arrow flew, skinning its flank.

Cedar did that thing she did so well. She noted the speed of the boar, its height, its weight, the angle of the spear, the height of the tip, the anchor behind her, the length of the spear, and then it was upon her.

She braced with all her might. Holding the spear in a vice grip, she lowered it just a fraction of an inch, and the boar hit the tip just below its left eye. Both the predator and the prey screamed as the boar shoved its way down the spear.

Cedar had no brake on this spear to stop its progress. She was counting on the pig running out of life before it reached her. It snarled and pawed its way forward pushing the spear deeper into its head. Cedar held on. She thought about Harken's knees pushing against her shoulders. And then the tip pierced the pig's cerebrum, and the creature dropped.

The predators held still, they looked like an odd sculpture in an art museum. Suddenly, the statue came to life. Harken touched Cedar's head. "That was close. Too close. Bravo," he whispered. She finally took a breath and withdrew the spear. It made a sucking sound as it exited the eye socket.

There was shouting and Flying Bird came rocketing through the undergrowth. "Come, come, Sol," he shouted in his new Lenape/English.

They raced after Flying Bird to find Sol lying in a bloody heap. A boar had torn a jagged gash across his lower abdomen. Three Stars was stuffing it with moss as Black Bear and Migwan fashioned a sling to carry him home.

Cedar and Harken knelt on each side of Sol and spoke softly to him. When they rolled him over onto the sling, he shrieked. Cedar put her face close to his. "You will be okay. I command it." She kissed him on the forehead. His face relaxed.

"I am the King of Kuts, I will survive," he whispered.

Now, a very different procession including an injured hunter and three dead pigs made its way in reverse to the safety of the village. Harken kept his hand on Sol's chest and Cedar kept her hand on his.

Blood dripped steadily from both predator and prey. Later that night, animals of all sorts would sniff that blood, and the droplets from the King of Kuts would make them nervous.

Harken thought about:

Sol-would he live?
the blood
the boar's eye
Cedar's hand on his

Cedar thought about:

Sol-he had to survive
Phoenix would know what to do
the boar's eye
Harken's hand

Chapter 28
Surgery

Everyone gathered around Sol. The King of Kut's breathing was shallow as if it hurt to take a deep breath. "Harken, quick get him on this bench. Cedar, go get Sol's pack, mine and the books. Katami, get that fire going." Phoenix barked out orders. She pulled her hair back in a knot and put water on to boil.

Harken opened *Netter's Illustrated Anatomy* to a cross section of the abdomen and positioned it so Phoenix could see. Cedar tossed the tools into the boiling water. "Harken, see what *Gray's Anatomy* has to say about wound repair. Read it out to me."

And so they stood, three travelers from another time attempting the impossible: Harken reading aloud, Cedar sterilizing the tools and Phoenix preparing to thread the needle in more ways than one.

Lenape healers went to work preparing their dressings and bandages as the novice surgical team washed their hands in the hot water. Flying Bird and Three Stars stood at each end, prepared to hold him down if needed.

They were ready. All were silent save Harken who read on. *"The two abdominal rectus muscles may be separated from their normal juxtaposition. With the abdomen relaxed..."*

Phoenix put her hand on Sol's skinny chest. Harken stopped reading and did the same along with Cedar. "Our future lies in the past," they chanted. And so Phoenix removed the moss and pulled back the jagged edges of the wound with something that looked like tongs. Cedar held the tongs in place as Phoenix poked around inside to see if there was any debris or as the book warned, severed arteries. "So, arteries are the ones that are pushing the blood around?"

"I think so. We have to see if blood is still oozing out." Harken leaned in closer. "What's that?"

"Maybe the intestine?"

"Damn, it's hard to see anything. Look, the picture shows the small intestine is right there."

Phoenix pressed around the edges. "I don't see a bleeder, but I could be wrong."

"Wait, what's that?" Phoenix took a tweezer and pulled out another piece of moss which revealed a gash in what they hoped was a muscle. She and Harken studied it. "Whatever it is, it's torn and bleeding."

Harken flipped through the pages. "Here, it's the rectus abdominis, maybe, hopefully."

"Damn, I better reattach that first and then hope for a miracle." Ever so gently, she washed the wound with hot water. Sol groaned and arched his back in pain. Three Stars knelt at the patient's feet and held his legs steady.

Flying Bird did the same but held Sol's arms crossed on his chest. Next, Phoenix threaded the curved needle with the sutures that Sol had taken from the hospital ruin. All eyes were on the surgeon. Her hand was steady, but her mind swirled in doubt. Phoenix took a deep breath and pushed the doubt aside. All her energy was focused on Sol. She could do this. She had to do it.

Cedar spoke quietly into Sol's ear reminding him of all the plans he had for his new life. The Lenape called on their spirits to heal Sol. Katami's baby turned and dropped. The river ran unimpeded to the sea, and the earth continued its orbit around the sun.

Phoenix studied the drawing one last time. Now, she had to act. The needle pierced the muscle, and she tugged the suture through connecting the two pieces. Sol yelped and squirmed. Sweat dripped from Phoenix's forehead. Twenty-eight stitches and an eternity later, the King of Kuts now had the biggest and nastiest scar to add to his collection, the lumpy gash ran from his belly button to his hip.

All stared at Phoenix's handy work. It wasn't pretty but at least the bleeding had stopped. Harken and Cedar wound the dressing around his waist and secured it in front. The surgical team stood quietly, unsure of what to do next. Just then, Dancing Fish spoke in low hushed tones. He was asking the spirits to help Sol and his friends. He raised both hands, and the tribe went to work moving Sol to the biggest wigwam where he would be watched day and night.

Drums beat out the story for all to hear of the Four Travelers from out of time. If the newcomers could understand, they would have heard for the first time, the story of the girl with sun in her hair and a ring in her nose. The story of Phoenix would evolve as she practiced her healing arts. She would come to be known as Little Sun.

Meanwhile, Phoenix dropped her arms to her sides and burst into tears. Harken gently took the needle from her, and Cedar held her tight. Phoenix burrowed her head into Cedar's shoulder and took deep breaths.

The tribe gathered around the makeshift surgery examining her work. They spoke in low soft tones, and many leaned down to whisper to Sol. Katami gently guided Phoenix to the river to bathe away the stress and the blood and the tears. Sol slept.

Chapter 29
Fever Dream

Sol struggled to open his eyes, and then he was sorry that he did. He stood on a cliff, his toes dangling over the edge. He forced himself to look down the hundreds of feet to a valley floor. His head snapped back. *Do not look. Move back from the edge.* His feet seemed disconnected from his brain. *What was he doing here? Why can't I move?*

Suddenly, a sharp pain shot down his spine, and he felt something erupting from his back. He turned his head to see huge wings unfolding their gooey white feathers to their full extent. *Wait, what is...* Before he could even wonder what was happening, he heard the wind speak to him in a language that was familiar yet strange. It seemed to be saying that it was too late, he had to jump.

His new wings stirred and fluttered as the insistent wind carved its way between each feather. Sol reached back to touch them. The wings rose up and as they descended, it lifted him just a few inches from the cliff's edge. He was falling or was he flying. Insistent currents pushed him this way and that. A flock of bright red birds flew around him. He followed them to the edge of the continent where he saw the sea touch the sky. The vastness of the ocean scared him, and he turned back. He was suddenly too aware of his predicament. And then, he was swimming in a river, his wings were gone. He dove beneath the glittering surface. How long could he hold his breath? Small fish flickered by, flashes of orange, green and purple. Big eyes peered out at him from beneath rocks and curling roots. One fish spoke. "Sol, are you awake? Sol, it's me, Phoenix."

Sol's eyes flew open.

Phoenix held his hand. "You're back!"

"You had a little run in with a pig." Harken put his hand on Sol's shoulder. "It's so good to see you awake again."

"You scared us. Damn it!" Cedar didn't realize how worried she was about him.

"I was flying and talking to fish," mumbled Sol.

"Cool dream." Cedar smiled.

"Scary dream."

And so, Sol recovered and his Lenape name, Many Scars, was born. Many Scars was very lucky. As it turned out, there were no bleeders or severed arteries and somehow the tusk did not puncture the intestine, but his rectus abdominis muscle did shorten, and the scar tissue build up pulled oddly at his side, a constant reminder of his brush with death.

Chapter 30
Love

Everyday Harken read aloud to an ever-growing audience from *Gray's Anatomy* and *Webster's Dictionary*, such unlikely texts. Most of what he read went in one ear and out the other, but he enjoyed the process, and the Lenape were not only entertained by it, they were also picking up some words here and there. Harken also loved to read aloud because Cedar liked to listen. She sat right next to him so she could follow along. Harken would lean against her shoulder and point to the words as he read.

To keep her next to him, he thought he could read forever. On most days, Sol joined Harken to work on the alphabet with Cedar and any other curious volunteers. Today, Cedar scrawled the 26 letters of the alphabet in the dirt all on her own.

"Nice work!" shouted Sol as he took off chasing two younger boys who had stolen his stick. The circle of rag tag students followed suit, and a game of chase ensued. Laughter and shrieks abounded as they tore around the village, stirring up dust and good cheer.

Harken and Cedar were left alone. Harken fiddled in the dirt with a stick. He watched it scratch out a message almost as if it wasn't his hand guiding it. *I think you are amazing!* Cedar glanced at Harken. His blue eyes sparked. She felt it. He pointed, indicating that she should try to read it.

At first, she hesitated. *What if she was wrong and sounded stupid?* But the warrior maiden rose up, and she began. Her voice softened as she worked out the last word. Both stood very still, too still perhaps because it was just enough time and enough stillness for both to feel the threads between them intertwine. Again, Cedar faced the blue eyes. "Write another."

Harken wrote, *Please teach me to hunt.* This one made her smile. Next, *I think your Lenape name should be, Silver Fox.* Cedar sounded it out faster this time.

Again, a big smile. "Yeah, that's a cool name." So, the lesson went on like this, sentence after sentence. Harken was trying to embolden himself to reveal that he liked her and had liked her ever since he saw her that first day, the girl with silver arms.

Suddenly, the words were there etched in the dirt. Had he written it? *I like you Silver Fox.* Slowly, she sounded it out. The world ground to a halt. Was he breathing? Did she laugh? It seemed like forever before Cedar moved.

This time, she didn't smile or laugh or speak. Instead, she took a stick and wrote her first words ever: *I like you* just below his message. Her face felt hot. Harken let his hand brush against hers and just like that, Cedar held on.

She didn't decide to hold his hand, it just happened. His hand felt rough and warm and kind. She stood taller and forced herself to look him in the eye. And so blue eyes mixed with brown or were they green as two kids, two time-travelers, two brains, two hearts, two visions joined up to seek a common future 400 years in the past.

Harken adjusted his grip on her hand. It felt lean and strong. The outside world seemed to disappear. Cedar felt a warm light meander up and down her arm, and she squeezed his hand. He squeezed back.

Cedar thought about:

kissing Harken
her new name
her first sentence
his warm hand

Harken thought about:

kissing Cedar

Chapter 31
The Birth

Katami's water broke early one morning beneath a waxing Planting Moon. In another time, a sonogram would have revealed that the baby was wedged tightly into an occiput posterior position which creates a difficult birth. A cesarean section might have been performed to prevent birth injuries, but it was 1600, and Phoenix and her crew had no idea why this birth ended in death the first time. They weren't even sure if this was the birth that they stumbled on the first time they arrived here. All they knew was that when Katami's time came, they would do everything possible to help.

Katami slipped out of her wigwam in the growing light as dawn raised its sleepy head. Stars still shone, the river sped to the sea, a Great Horned Owl hooted its five notes, and a rabbit ran for cover.

Silently, she entered Phoenix's wigwam and touched her shoulder. Phoenix shot awake. Suddenly, her new home was a stir with activity.

"Sol, you get the bag of medical stuff, Harken the books. Cedar, you get the fire going and boil the instruments. This is it."

"We can do this, hands in." Cedar stuck out her hand and three piled on top.

"Our future lies in the past," they chanted.

"Go wake White Otter and Sly Turtle." Phoenix created a pallet for Katami who was pacing.

Once again, Phoenix called upon her emerging super power. She was learning to put aside reality and take action under extreme difficulties. In this case, reality was that she knew almost nothing about childbirth, and yet this hard fact didn't affect her. Her super power locked it up in a dark place, and she proceeded as if she knew it would be okay. In preparation, Harken had read and reread the obstetrics sections of their tiny library consisting of two books aloud to them but there was no substitute for experience.

They had studied the intricate illustrations, growing comfortable with looking at body parts of all kinds. The human body was just another miracle of nature. Briefly, Phoenix wondered why people in the future were so uncomfortable with the naked body. A groan from Katami brought her back to the moment.

Katami was hunched over with a hand on her side. Phoenix slipped her arm through hers, lifting her to a standing position and with a little bit of encouragement, they set off to walk laps around the village fire pit. Katami chanted as they walked, the pitch crescendoing at the height of each contraction.

Harken followed along behind them, babbling on about how far apart the contractions were. "What do you think Phoenix, should we check to see if she is dilated?" He started to count the seconds between the highest notes of Katami's chant. "One, two, three…"

Cedar leaned over the hot fire and stared into the water about to boil. Her reflection quivered as the water heated up. *Is that me*, she thought, *the girl who likes Harken?* Just saying his name felt good somehow. She dumped all the tools into the boiling water and stirred them a bit. Sol arrived with an armload of wood and disappeared to get more. He was happiest with a task at hand. Cedar watched him go and noticed his spine curled just a bit to the right side, still guarding his newest wound.

Rays of sunlight sent the mist on its way, the village stirred. The villagers stopped to give Katami encouragement and then went about their day. Gray Wolf came to Katami and spoke, laying his hands on each side of her belly. She grabbed both hands and held them tightly. He spoke again, and she answered in hushed tones. Phoenix stood by in silence, drinking it in. Katami's chosen mate was from the Turtle Clan and she, the Wolf Clan.

Nearby, Sly Turtle ground up some sumac and sassafras roots to make a pain-relieving tea while White Otter flipped through the anatomy pictures one more time. She and a few others had become very interested and spent a lot of time studying this new information.

White Otter, a wise Lenape healer, ran her pointer finger over the illustration of the baby curled up inside the mother. If her IQ could have been tested, it would reveal that she was extremely gifted, genius perhaps. Her finger came to a stop at the cervix where the baby would have to make a turn. She already knew that Katami's baby was facing the wrong way or the harder way. Her hand spun as if she was practicing turning the baby.

She realized that this one had his or her head pushed up against this little circle Harken called a cervix in a way that would force him (she thought it was a boy) to arch his head back to make the turn. She made soft grunting sounds as she thought about this short journey of just six inches that was so difficult. Perhaps she would try something new this time. She positioned the open book beside the pallet.

The hours dragged by with no baby because just as both Phoenix and White Otter thought, the baby was turned the wrong way. Cedar and Sol kept the fire going and the instruments boiling. Harken studied the birth positions. Phoenix paced. She knew it was time. She had to check if the cervix was opening.

She gently coaxed Katami into position on the makeshift cot. Sly Turtle massaged her temples, and Katami closed her eyes. Phoenix tied her hair back and stuck her hands in the hot water, White Otter did the same.

Phoenix stood between Katami's legs and raised her knees. She massaged her lower legs for a bit and then pushed her knees to the side. There was the door to the baby. Again she immersed her hands in the hot water and then White Otter greased them up with what she wasn't sure.

Phoenix took a deep breath and listened one more time to Harken reading about checking the cervix. And then she gently pushed her right hand through the opening. The canal squeezed her hand, she pushed a little farther.

"Can you feel the cervix?" Harken's voice was shrill.

"I'm at the end of the canal, I think. I'm not sure what I'm feeling. Wait, oh wow, I feel the head. The cervix must be open."

"See how many fingers you can get in the opening." Katami writhed and pulled back from the pressure. Sly Turtle chanted with her through the pain. Soon, there was a chorus of chants as others joined in to help.

"All my fingers fit. It's open." She gently felt the head. Was that hair? And then a contraction happened, and she felt the head move a bit toward Katami's back. It all made sense now, she felt how the baby's position caused the contractions to push the head past the open doorway.

She withdrew her hand and consulted with White Otter and Harken. "Let's see if a new position will help. I think maybe she should get on her hands and knees for a bit." Slowly, they coaxed Katami into this position. The day wore on and Katami paced, knelt, squatted but no baby. She was losing strength and holding onto Phoenix's hand like a vice.

White Otter changed tactics and stood over Katami, lightly massaging her belly. She located the baby's feet and back as she worked, and tried to turn him. She wondered if Phoenix could push the head back in a bit, would he turn.

Harken was thinking the same thing. "What if you push the head back in, the baby might turn. We've got to do something."

And so she did. "I don't think it's working." Phoenix's face was in a knot. Katami was chanting louder and louder. White Otter continued to massage the baby in a circular motion.

"What about using these?" Sol held up the forceps. "They look like they're made for the job."

Katami had been in labor for many hours, and now the sun was setting. She had lost track of where she ended and the pain began. All was misery. The light at the end of the tunnel was going out.

Phoenix grabbed the forceps. She mimed how she would use them for all to see and White Otter nodded her head. The long tong-like instrument slipped in easily. Katami dug her nails into the cot and chanted louder and faster.

The women of the tribe were all watching now and they joined in. The sound of their chanting held them together, made them one. Phoenix rose up above it all and looked down on herself, her friends, and her new family. The chant swirled around her, empowered her. They had to succeed.

She opened the forceps and ever so gently twirled them until she thought they might be around the head. Harken read aloud about proper forceps use. She heard, "Wait for a contraction and then apply…" The contraction arrived. Katami arched her back. White Otter pushed hard from the outside world. Phoenix twisted and tugged gently on the inside world. "Pull harder, just go for it."

Tears arrived. Phoenix took a deep breath and pulled. White Otter pushed harder. The inside world shifted; the baby turned a little. Was it enough? The tears blurred Phoenix's vision.

The next contraction came immediately, pushing the baby down the canal and Phoenix pulled the forceps out. "The head is crowning!" shouted Harken. He was getting the terminology down. Cedar and Sol held their breath. White Otter whispered to Katami. The tribe gathered at a distance.

One more contraction produced a tiny head with the shoulders quickly following. Together, Phoenix and

Harken, caught the slippery little guy. White Otter had guessed correctly. They placed the baby on Katami's chest. She cradled him to her breast, tears came. He whimpered.

Mother and baby took their first look at each other. Gently, Katami touched the marks the forceps had made. White Otter bit the cord and proceeded to see to the afterbirth. The tribe gave a collective sigh of relief and gathered closer to see their new member. Gray Wolf sat next to Katami and touched his son.

The travelers from another world looked down on this scene for the second time, but this time there were smiles all around. Harken took Cedar's hand, and she took hold of Sol's who found Phoenix's.

Four interlopers in a strange, new world. All had tears, tears of joy and tears of wonder. Harken squeezed Cedar's hand, and she passed it along. "Our future lies in the past," they whispered. And so the Universe shifted and made room for both mother and son this time around.

As was Lenape custom, Dancing Fish came to pay his respects and welcome the infant. His soft voice instructed the drummers to begin, and he spoke. Dusk dressed him in a soft glowing light as he raised his hands and told the tale of the four travelers from far, far away who came to them with strange new ways.

He spoke of Many Scars, the teacher; Silver Fox, the hunter; Wind in his Hair, the storyteller; and Little Sun, the healer. He suggested that this was a special baby to be guided into the world by these four strangers with books and knowledge from another time.

He thanked nature for this healthy soul and proclaimed the four as the infant's spirit guides. Then he very carefully enfolded the fragile new life in his big strong hands and lifted him up to the now rising moon. The tiny newcomer cooed softly, and his skinny arms reached out, quivering.

At this very moment just beyond the trees, a great wooden ship, the *Half Moon,* a Dutch clipper, sailed up the river for the first time. It was 1609. The Captain, Henry Hudson, and his crew stood wide-eyed taking in this lush new world, new to them.